Search
for a
Kiwi Killer

DES HUNT

Search
for a
Kiwi Killer

DES HUNT

 Torea Press

First published 2018 by Torea Press
107 Miro Place, RD2 Whitianga 3592, New Zealand
© Des Hunt 2018
ISBN978-0-9941226-6-7

A catalogue record for this book is available from the National Library of New Zealand.

Design: Des Hunt — www.deshunt.com
Editor: Donna Blaber — www.donnablaber.com
Cover: Des Hunt
Cover Images:
   Forest Scene — Irantzu Arbaizagoitia — creativemarket.com
   Dog — Foxery Digital — creativemarket.com
   Dead Kiwi — Todd Hamilton — backyardkiwi.org.nz
   All others — Des Hunt
Printer: Asia Pacific Offset

1

Pig on the Run

Tom Smart had been waiting on the corner for ages, more than an hour at least. Looking back down the road, he saw that all the other kids from school had gone. Only a row of cars remained. *Teachers having an end of term party,* he thought. *No use going there to ring Dad.*

He'd known since that morning there'd be problems. "Don't take the bus," his father had said. "I'll pick you up straight after school. We might have to make a trip."

Tom had been no happier then than he was now. This was what he'd expected. It was so typical of Brandon Smart – 'straight after' could be any time up to three hours. Then, when he did arrive, there'd be all sorts of excuses to explain the lateness – always somebody else's fault, never his own.

Tom sighed, wondering if he had time to go down the road to the takeaways. He probably had enough money for a drink. He'd even taken a few steps in that direction when yelling from further up the road caught his attention. Turning, he saw two kids chasing some animal towards him.

A pig?

Yes! It was! Not a monster, a young one, like a Labrador dog with short legs. Small enough for a boy to catch. That's if he could run fast enough. The two who were after it certainly weren't. They were screaming for help. "Tom! Tom! Block it off!" yelled Sean the older of the two.

"Grab it, if you can," added Luke, the other kid in pursuit.

Dropping his school bag, Tom moved into the middle of the road waving his arms. The pig was now only seconds away, heading straight at him. All Tom had to do was stay there and he'd have it. Then a car horn blasted: loud, close, and scary. Tom jumped to the side. A car sped past, abusive words spewing from the window.

At the same time, the pig rushed past on the other side.

"No you don't," growled Tom, turning to give chase.

"Go Tom!" yelled Sean.

Tom went.

By then the pig had a lead of 20 metres, sprinting down the middle of Cobham Road, one of the busiest streets in Kerikeri. Cars pulled over, others veered, some towards the pig. Most had horns blasting at both the animal and its pursuer.

Tom was fast and fresh. The pig was tired and slowing. A service lane must have looked darker and safer, for the pig moved into it, seeking a refuge from the mayhem. Tom swerved to follow, his feet skidding on the gravel before accelerating off, only ten metres behind.

Down the alley raced Tom, closing in on the exhausted pig. But the pig was smart, and when it saw a gap between two buildings that was just wide enough for a pig, it took it. Tom didn't even try to follow. He kept going down the lane, knowing there was an exit beside the cinema. Now it all depended on which way the animal went when it got through to Hobson Avenue.

The pig got it wrong, turning towards the business end, close to where Tom would reappear. They were on a collision course.

When Tom burst out of the alleyway, he was within two metres of the pig who quickly took a tight turn into the service station on the corner.

That was the pig's second mistake. New concrete had recently been laid in the forecourt. Concrete that the owners kept clean and shiny. That made it great for car tyres, but hopeless for pig trotters. When the pig tried to turn between the pumps it kept going, crashing into a windscreen-washing bucket. Tom was on top in a flash and they slid across the forecourt until an ice freezer got in the way, stopping them with a thud.

Although the pig looked exhausted, that didn't stop it voicing its anger at being caught. Who would have thought a pig could make so much noise? The squeals echoed around the forecourt drowning out the sounds of the people who were gathering around.

Still Tom held on, both arms around the pig's neck, each holding a front leg.

"Keep it there," said a voice from over his shoulder, "while I hogtie it with this."

Tom looked up to see a guy bending over with a bungee cord. Soon all four legs of the pig were tied together and the guy was standing back staring down at the pig, his face split by a huge grin as if he'd just won the calf-roping contest at a rodeo.

Ten minutes later the pig was lying quietly on the concrete. Sean, Luke, Tom, and three adult males gathered around. The discussion centred around whether the pig was one from a pig farm up on the main road or a wild one that had come down out of Waitangi Forest. Mike, the guy who had hogtied the animal, reckoned it was wild.

"It's this drought," he said, "they're having trouble finding water. They're coming out of the forest. Last week I saw a couple on the side of Inlet Road, scratching around in the drain in broad daylight. I tell you, they're starving." He pointed at the pig. "Anyway Rob McKenzie's pigs have better breeding than that. It's a feral for sure."

"What are we going to do with it?" asked another. "Eat it?"

Mike turned to Tom. "You caught it, so it's your pig. What do you want to do?"

Tom was taken aback. "Um … I don't know … ah … what would you do?"

"Return it to the forest. She's a sow. A couple of months and she'll be ready to breed."

"Be good eating, but," said the other guy.

"Yeah, but you don't want to eat the sows, especially not the … young … ones." His attention swapped to a woman approaching the group. "Hello Marika," he said, smiling broadly. "You here for a story."

"Hi Mike. Heard someone had caught a pig. Thought I'd better take a look. It's not every day you get a pig running through Kerikeri. Did you catch it?"

"Nah. Young lad here caught it." He pointed to Tom. "Pig came screaming down the road with the boy in hot pursuit. Took it in a perfect tackle as it tried to cut though here. All I did was tie it up."

While he was speaking, Marika had taken a notebook out of her bag and started writing. "Is it a feral or domestic?"

"Has to be feral, Marika," replied Mike. "It came from the direction of the forest, not Rob McKenzie's place."

Marika asked a few more questions – gender, estimated weight, age – before turning to Tom. "Can I have your name, please?"

Tom gave it.

"Okay, now I need a photo. Can we move the pig out so that I get a better background." Then, after that was done she said, "Right, now, if you'll crouch down beside it Tom, I'll take a snap."

"No!" said a loud voice from the other side of the forecourt. "No photo!"

Everyone turned to look at the source, a tall, muscular man, arms covered in tattoos. While the others stared, Tom groaned and looked away. He knew what would come next.

"Why not, sir?" asked Marika.

"Because Tom doesn't want his photo taken. He doesn't want his name in the paper either."

Marika's eyes narrowed. "And what gives you the right to make decisions for the boy?"

"I'm his father, Brandon Smart. And who are you?"

"Marika Greenwell from the *Northland Informer*. Why doesn't Tom want his name and photo in the paper?"

"Because it'll give him a swollen head."

Marika turned her face away. trying not to laugh. A couple of the others couldn't hold back their sniggers. Tom knew it was time to step in before his father made more of a fool of himself.

"It shouldn't be my photo," he said. "Sean and Luke found the pig and did all the hard work. I was just lucky at the end. If you take their photo you can have a person each side."

This appealed to Marika. The attention shifted away from Brandon and Tom to the other boys. Names were recorded, stories told, photos taken. After that Marika left, as did most of the others until the only ones remaining were the boys, Mike, Brandon, and the pig.

"C'mon Tom, time to go," said Brandon.

"What about the pig?" asked Mike. "What do you want done with it?"

Brandon looked blank.

Tom stepped in. "We'll take it and put it back in the forest." He turned to Sean and Luke. "Do you want to come?"

"Nah," said Luke. "We came to see a movie so we'd better get over there."

Brandon's van was parked a few strides away, half blocking the forecourt. Mike carried the pig over and dumped it in the back where seats had been removed to make room for a mattress. The animal seemed quite relaxed about things.

"What about the bungee?" asked Brandon. "Is that yours?"

"Keep it," said Mike. "I've got dozens of them." A pause. "Do you know your way around the forest?"

"Some of it."

"There's a pond off the main track. Have you been there?"

Brandon shook his head.

"I have," said Tom. "I can show him."

"Well, I think there's still some water in there," said Mike. "Drop the pig near that and maybe it'll have a chance of surviving." He slowly shook his head. "But if this drought continues, I don't hold out much hope. It'll be hard enough keeping farm animals alive. The wild ones won't stand a chance."

2

Waitangi Forest

Nothing was said as the panel van rattled out of town. No excuses from Brandon. No accusations from Tom. Nothing from the pig either. Maybe the animal sensed it was on its way to freedom.

The way to the forest was also the way home: along Cobham onto Inlet Road, passing orange and mandarin orchards until it dropped down to cross an estuary. On the other side, a posh subdivision was under development on the left, with the start of Waitangi Forest on the right. The track to Brandon and Tom's place was on the edge of the forest, hidden from view by overhanging trees.

Instead of turning towards home, Brandon continued one more kilometre to a second entrance into the forest. This one was much more obvious with several signs saying what you could and couldn't do if you entered. The track was part of Te Araroa Trail, a walkway that stretched the length of New Zealand from Cape Reinga in the north, to Bluff in the south. This bit covered the 20 kilometres from Kerikeri to the Treaty Grounds at Waitangi.

"Turn off here," said Tom, his first words since leaving the service station.

"I know," said Brandon.

"Back there you said you didn't know."

"I know where to turn off, I just don't know where the pond is exactly."

Tom let him settle into driving on the rough narrow track before going on the attack.

"Did you contact Mum?"

"Yeah, that's why I was late. She went on and on about things." A pause. "Like she always does."

"So what's happening to me over the holidays?"

Brandon glanced over to his son. "She doesn't want you."

Tom turned to stare out the side window. Part of him was pleased he didn't have to spend two weeks with his mum, the partner, and their new kid. He'd been with them for most of January and it had been real bad: the only time either adult spoke to him was to complain about how he was upsetting the baby. Everyone was relieved when he returned to his father for the start of school.

And yet another part of him was sad that she didn't want him. In movies and TV programmes mums were the ones who loved their children most. While his said she did, there were few visible signs. On the other hand, although Brandon would never use the word 'love', he did try to do the right thing, at least as he saw it. The problem was the authorities had decided that Tom should live with his mother, Mandy, which meant what they were doing was illegal.

"Does she know where we are?"

"Nope. She mentioned Auckland, so I suppose she thinks we're still there."

Tom nodded to himself. *That's why no names and photos.*

"Have you got any work for the next two weeks?"

"Yeah. The early fruit is ready for picking. I'll be flat out."

Tom smiled. That meant he could do whatever he wanted during the holidays. That was much, much better than being with his mum.

"But you can stop smiling," continued Brandon. "I'm arranging for Dave to look after you when I'm not there."

The smile vanished. "Aw, Dad. Why him?"

"Because he's close by."

"But I don't need anybody to look after me!"

"How old are you?"

"Eleven."

"Right. Then the law says you do. I don't want the authorities coming around because you've got yourself

15

into trouble. I've got enough to worry about already. Dave Hughes will be looking after you and that's that."

From then on the only living sound inside the van was a grunt every now and then from the pig.

They passed from large mature pine trees ready for felling, into an area that had recently been cleared and lay waiting for replanting when the rains returned. No use releasing the pig there as no animal, whether insect, bird or mammal, would survive in that grey wasteland.

Continuing on, there were further blocks of trees before they came to a turnoff.

"Hold it!" said Tom. "We've gone too far. Turn around."

"I didn't see any pond."

'It's back there, hidden in the trees. You need to turn around."

As Brandon slipped the gear stick into reverse, he asked, "How come you know the forest so well? Do you run this far?"

"Nah. I've ridden this way a couple of times."

"When?"

"After school," said Tom, before adding the barb. "When I'm waiting for you to come home."

"Tom, I *do* need some sort of social life. It's not like I—"

"Stop!" interrupted Tom. "There it is. Wow, that's changed from last time I was here. No wonder I missed it. The water's almost gone."

They got a clearer look when the van had been backed up a bit. Between some drooping ferns was a small pond surrounded by cracked mud. A pair of ducks swimming in the remaining water eyed them warily.

"Okay, let's get Miss Piggy," said Brandon, climbing out of the van. "Time for her to return to the wild."

At first it seemed as if Miss Piggy wasn't too keen to leave the comfort of the mattress. Only when Brandon grabbed a leg did she show any interest in the two humans. Still there was no struggling, as if she accepted whatever fate they had in store.

That lasted until she was placed on the ground beside the water. Now, exactly when they wanted her to be calm, she fought to be free, making it impossible to remove the bungee. In the end Brandon took out a pocket knife and cut it. The bungee flew off and so did Miss Piggy, flying across the mud and into the undergrowth below the pines. In an instant she was out of sight.

"Can't have been thirsty," said Tom.

"She'll be back," said Brandon. "Look at all the prints."

Hundreds of trotter holes in the mud showed the pond was an important watering hole for pigs of all sizes.

"Wow!" said Tom. "That's a lot of pigs."

"Or a few pigs returning many times."

Tom moved towards the pond where the mud was still soft. "There's been birds as well. See."

"That's a big bird," said Brandon. "Bigger than a pukeko, I would think."

"Kiwi," said Tom.

"You reckon so?"

"I know so." Tom pointed to the other side of the pond. "There it is." A fluffy brown mass crouched on the mud, its beak slightly buried. "Looks like it's sick.

"Let's take a look."

Before they got around to the other side, they knew the kiwi was more than sick. It was dead and judging by the stink, had been that way for a day or so.

"Could it have starved?" asked Tom.

Instead of answering, Brandon touched the kiwi with his foot. The carcass fell sideways exposing a crawling mass of maggots.

"Yuk!" yelled Tom.

"Didn't starve to death. Some animal has ripped into its leg."

As the maggots crawled away from the light, a long wound became exposed stretching from the bare part of the leg up to the top of the thigh.

"Would a pig do that?"

"Doubt it. Has to be a dog."

Tom thought about that. "But it could have been after the kiwi died, couldn't it?"

Brandon shook his head. "If it was after food, then it

would have eaten much more than that. No, this bird was killed by a dog. Looks like we've got a kiwi killer around here, somewhere."

Tom stood and let his eyes scan around the site, wondering if the animal was watching them. If it was, then it must have been well hidden. But still, the thought of a killer dog worried him. He ran and rode through this forest all the time. He'd caught glimpses of animals in the past and not thought much about it. Now he realised he could have been seeing a dog. A vicious killer. One who might just as easily attack him as it would a kiwi.

"You won't see it," said Brandon. "Probably hunts at night when the owner thinks it's sleeping."

"Might be a wild dog."

"Nah. I'd agree with that if more of the kiwi was eaten, but this killer wasn't hungry. It gets a good feed at home. It kills for the fun of it." After that, he began walking back to the van. "C'mon Tom, let's get home. This forest gives me the spooks."

3

Home

The hut that Brandon called home sat between the forest and the estuary. The renting agency called it a 'rural beach bach'. The 'beach' was a six-by-one-metre strip of sand that separated the grassy bank from the mud of the estuary. The only time any sea water lapped upon that sand was during king tides. At other times the water was hidden by the mangrove forest that filled all except a narrow channel of the estuary.

Nor was the 'rural' description all that accurate either, as the scrubland that separated the estuary from the forest was far from productive farmland. But the bach part was right, if you considered a bach as having the bare basics for survival. This one had two rooms: a living area with kitchen at one end, table and lounge furniture at the other, and a bedroom with two sets of up-and-down bunks and a wardrobe. Under a lean-to out the back was a shower and tub. The toilet was a long-drop hidden in the scrub. While it wasn't much of a place, it was better than living in the van, which they'd done in the past.

The weekend passed by much the same as they always did: Brandon resting up after working in the orchards all week, Tom watching TV or simply messing about. Not until Sunday afternoon did they do anything out of the ordinary.

After his lunchtime snooze, Brandon came into the living area where Tom was watching a movie. "C'mon you. We need to go and see Dave. I want to get the holiday arrangements sorted."

Tom groaned. "Do I have to? Can't I stay and watch this?"

"No," said Brandon grabbing the remote. "You're coming too."

This time Tom's groan was louder.

Dave Hughes's bach was a short distance up the estuary. A dirt path between the two was wildly overgrown except where Brandon had pushed the weeds back on previous trips to see his neighbour. Only once before had Tom been with him.

Although the two baches had the same basic design, Dave's looked more like a home than a hut. A mown patch of lawn stretched down to the estuary, flowering shrubs lined the front of the building, and its yellow and orange paint job glowed in the summer sun. A welcoming place, apart from a sign facing the estuary:

PRIVATE LAND
NO ENTRY

A dinghy leaning against the post, pointed towards a pathway of mud through the mangroves. *Maybe he'll let me use it,* thought Tom, his mood brightening. Then he saw there was only one oar and his spirits sunk. That single oar in the stern was a reminder of why he'd avoided coming back after his first visit. Tom steeled himself for what he knew was coming.

His father knocked on the door.

At first glance the man who appeared seemed no different to most other men in their late fifties. There were the required number of wrinkles, enough to get an idea of his age. The greying hair hadn't receded too much, and yes, his belly did protrude over his belt, but not grossly so. There was nothing there that would upset Tom. That was still hidden.

Not for long though. When Dave saw who it was, he opened the door widely, inviting them in. That's when the deformity became visible. Dave's left arm was missing. Not all of it. Most of the upper part remained, finishing in a rounded stump which Dave could waggle around like a motorized joystick. *That* was what caused Tom difficulties. He couldn't take his eyes off it. Whenever he looked at Dave, his eyes would automatically drop to stare at the stump.

"Come in, come in," said Dave. "I've just made a pot of tea."

Tom hadn't been inside before. While the design was the same as their place, it looked strikingly different. Yes, the furniture was better and everything was tidier, but it was the wall decorations that were most noticeable. On the back wall, three large photographs hung each side of a mounted animal head, a massive boar with long tusks curving up from an open jaw.

"Wow!" said Tom, his eyes wide.

Dave chuckled. "He always does that to people when they see him for the first time."

"He looks so real."

"Yeah, the taxidermist did a good job. Just as well, it cost me enough."

"Did you kill it?"

A nod.

"Do you still go …," began Tom, before realising what he was saying.

"No, I don't hunt now," said Dave, with a smile. He waggled the stump. "It's a bit hard with only one arm."

To hide his embarrassment, Tom said, "Those tusks are real sharp."

"Yes. Rip your gut open if you're not careful. An animal like that could kill you."

That gave Tom a thought. "Could it kill a kiwi?"

"Mmm. Probably, but I don't see why it would want to. Why do you ask?"

They sat down then while Tom and Brandon told the story of Miss Piggy, and finding the dead kiwi.

"Well, I can tell you two things," said Dave, when they'd finished. "One, that kiwi wasn't killed by a pig. If it had been, you'd only find feathers, nothing else. Anyway I've spent most of my life working in that forest. I've seen lots of pigs and I've seen lots of kiwi. A pig might eat a dead kiwi but I've not known them to kill one." He paused. "And the other thing is I wouldn't have returned that sow to the forest, not at the moment. Kiwi and pigs compete for food which must be getting short. When the rains come the pigs can recover quickly enough, but the kiwis can't. One less pig might have saved a couple of kiwis."

"What would you have done?" asked Tom.

"Eaten it. A young sow like that would be great eating. Too late now though." He turned to Brandon. "Tell me, how's your water supply holding out?"

Tom tuned out. He knew the water supply wasn't great, because it was mentioned every time he took a shower. He'd offered to stop washing, which hadn't gone down well. The drought didn't worry him. As far as he was concerned, day after day of cloudless sunshine was how the weather ought to be.

After a while he got up to study the photos. The three on the left were about pig hunting. Right alongside the mounted head was a photo of the pig shortly after it had been shot. A younger, two-armed Dave Hughes was crouched beside it. The animal was a monster. *A killer*, thought Tom. The next photo had three pigs, and two people; one of them was Dave. The other guy was also in the next photo, along with Dave, a couple of dogs, and yet another pig.

The photos on the other side were all about logging: monstrous machines, tall trees, and workers in safety gear. One was a group photo. Tom tried to make out Dave, but they all looked much the same in their outfits. He already knew Dave had lost his arm in a logging accident and wondered if this might be the place where it happened. One thing was sure, he wasn't going to ask the man. That stump troubled Tom enough already without starting a discussion about it.

These thoughts were broken by his father calling him.

"Hey Tom, come over here. Dave wants to lay down some ground rules."

The rules were simple enough. Tom had to check in with Dave three times a day: after Brandon went to work, again at lunch time, and at five o'clock when he would hang around until Brandon picked him up. If he left the area at any time he had to tell Dave where he was going and what he was doing. When asked if he was prepared to abide by these rules, Tom shrugged and said, "Yeah, they're okay," thinking they left him more than enough time to do his own thing.

They went into town for pizza that night which was not surprising, it had become something of a Sunday night ritual. As usual Tom was dropped at the pizza place while Brandon went and 'took care of some business'; stuff Tom wasn't allowed to ask about.

After placing the usual order – a meat-lovers and a Hawaiian – Tom went to sit down. The only chair available had a free newspaper sitting on it, almost like it was reserved. He looked around and seeing no one, picked up the paper and sat. He was about to put the paper under the seat when a photo on the front page caught his eye – a dead kiwi looking exactly like the one they'd found by the pond. This one also had a wound along the leg. A heading above the photo read:

KIWI KILLER ATTACKS AT KERIKERI

The text said that four dead kiwis had been found on Inlet Road in the past two weeks. Department of

Conservation (DoC) rangers had identified the wounds had been made by a dog. DoC were keen to hear of any other deaths. They were urging all dog owners to keep their dogs under control at all times. Everyone was reminded that kiwis had a peculiar smell that most dogs found attractive. They needed aversion training until they disliked the smell. Hunters were informed they were not allowed to take dogs into Northland forests unless they had a valid Aversion Training Certificate (ATC), and ATC's needed renewing every three months. DoC were also considering taking DNA samples from all dogs along Inlet Road so that they might find a match with DNA taken from the wounds of the dead kiwis.

Tom was considering this when he heard his name being called. He stood thinking the pizzas were ready. They weren't. It was Mike, the guy who had hogtied the pig.

"You having pizza for dinner as well?"

Tom nodded.

"Yeah, we do too, every Sunday," said Mike. "Did you get that sow back to the forest?"

"Yes. She didn't hang around for a drink, but. Ran off into the trees."

"She'll get back to it."

"Yeah, there were trotter marks all through the mud," said Tom. He thought for a moment before adding, "And kiwi tracks as well." He held up the newspaper. "We found one of these there."

Mike glanced at the paper and nodded as if he'd seen it already. "A dead kiwi in as far as the pond, eh? That's a bit worrying. You need to tell DoC about that. Or," he added, pointing to the paper, "Marika Greenwell. She'd pass it on."

Tom looked away.

"Okay, okay," said Mike. "I get it. Your dad won't let you do that. Tell you what, I'll do it for you. Will that be all right?"

It was.

"You know," said Mike after a time, "we had another crop of killings a few years back on the same road. Well, Wharau Road which is an extension of Inlet Road. Seven were found dead that time."

"Did they get the dog?"

"They put down three dogs that had been running free."

"Did the killing stop?"

"Yeah."

"Why did they put the dogs down? Why didn't they use this aversion training?" asked Tom, stabbing his finger at the paper.

Mike shook his head slowly. "That doesn't work on a dog once they start killing. The only way to stop it is to kill them. A bullet through the head does the job nicely. They don't kill any more kiwis after that, do they?"

Tom had no answer for this, and the conversation died. Soon afterwards his name was called, this time it was for the pizzas. He collected them and moved outside to wait for his dad, knowing from past experience, he could be waiting for a long time.

4

Shapes in the Forest

Brandon left for work at seven o'clock Monday morning, hoping to start picking while the temperature was cool. He woke Tom before he left.

"You don't need to go over to Dave's until nine. Let him have a sleep in. But make sure you do go over, right?"

Tom said he would, before rolling over, expecting to fall asleep. But that didn't happen and in the end he decided to go for a run. It would help him plan his day.

Tom had been only seven years old when he'd first started running . His parents were still living together then, although no longer happily. They argued endlessly. At first Tom would hide away, covering his ears trying to shut out the loud, bickering voices. Then one day it got so bad that he ran outside, crying. And he kept on running. After a few minutes the crying had stopped. After quarter of an hour he was feeling much better. When he did return home, half an hour later, he found the fighting had ended. In his absence, their anger had turned into concern, not for each other, but for him. From then on, he always went running.

Nowadays he ran because he was good at it. A couple of weeks before, he had cleaned up his age-group races for 800 metre and 1,500 metre at the Mid-North Athletics Champs. Coming up soon were the cross-country champs, which he also hoped to win. Later in the year he was planning to do the junior triathlon if he could get his cycling and swimming up to standard. That's if he still lived in Kerikeri which couldn't be guaranteed.

Living next to the forest had helped his running a lot. Within a minute of leaving the house he could be on a track surrounded by tall trees. Some of the tracks were logging roads, others were firebreaks. Most of the surfaces were good enough for running, so long as you kept an eye on where you were putting your feet.

On this day Tom was more aware of his surroundings than usual. He chose the smoother roads so he could keep a lookout for anything that might be nearby in the forest. He couldn't get the idea of a killer dog out of his head. He'd always been scared of dogs, especially when running, as many would rush at him, barking and snarling. While he'd never been bitten, that could easily change if there was a killer on the loose.

Of course, in this state of raised awareness, his imagination took over. A fallen log became a huge pig; a dark shrub turned into a black dog; every shadow was a hiding place.

"Don't be so stupid," he told himself. "There's nothing there." Which did little other than making the shadows more threatening.

The middle point for this run was a big open space where logging trucks could turn around. Cut logs had been arranged in the centre to form a roundabout, a place where he could sit and catch his breath. Today it had an added advantage: if there was an animal out there, it was at least 20 metres away.

As his breathing slowed, the sounds of the forest became more noticeable. Nearby were the chirps of small birds feeding in the ferns. From higher up came the songs of thrushes and blackbirds. Behind them all were distant noises of a logging operation in another part of the forest. Chainsaws, loaders, and the piercing air-horns they used to communicate with each other.

But there was also another sound, one Tom had not heard before. A whining, like that made by high-speed power tools.

"A dentist drill?" he asked himself, then chuckled at how stupid that was. "No Tom. They don't have dentists out here."

After that he couldn't hear it for a while. When the sound did come back, it was louder. Now he was able to work out what it was. A dog. Not the noise a killer would make; the whine of an animal in pain.

What should he do? His instinct said to run, but his curiosity urged him to find out more.

Getting to his feet, he moved towards the edge of the circle in the direction of the sound. He paused to listen. It was coming from within a group of tree ferns, well off the track. This was the dangerous part. If the animal was vicious, then Tom was moving into a position where flight would be difficult. Regardless, he moved forward.

The whining stopped.

So too did Tom, his heart thumping.

When the sound resumed it was a brief, lower-pitched, pleading call.

"It's all right," he said softly.

This time he saw a movement between the lower fronds. Reaching out, he pulled a branch back to get a clearer look. Yes, it was a dog, staring at him with frightened eyes.

"It's all right," Tom repeated. "I'm here to help."

The dog replied with more pleading whines.

Tom pushed between the fronds until he was just a few metres away. If the dog was going to attack it would do so now. Then he saw it couldn't attack. It was tied to fallen pine branch. He took another step. No, the animal wasn't tied, it was trapped by its collar.

The collar was thicker than most Tom had seen. Somehow, it had slipped over the broken end of the fallen branch, pinning the dog. In its struggles to get free, the dog had forced the collar over a twig, which then locked it in position, stopping any movement backwards and forwards. Unless Tom did something, the dog would stay there until it died.

The question was, would the dog let him set it free? There was only one way to find out. Tom took the last few steps until he was standing right by it. Now he could see the collar had a box attached, with a bit sticking up like an aerial. The two dogs in Dave's photo had similar things. A green LED on the side of the box was glowing.

"You a pig-hunting dog?" said Tom, touching the dog's head. "You get caught chasing a pig? Well let's see if we can get you free."

Tom's first thought was to break off the twig and ease the dog backwards. But a closer look showed that would cause the dog immense pain. Already its neck and shoulder were raw and clotted from rubbing against the branch. Moving in either direction would be agony. Fortunately the buckle was on the side away from the branch. Release that and the dog would be free.

Except it wasn't easy. The moment he put pressure on the collar, the dog yelped.

"Sorry fella," he said stroking the dog's back. "But I've got to do this."

Maybe the dog understood or, more likely, it was close to passing out. Either way, Tom was able to unbuckle the lead without further yelping. Only when he took it off did the dog make a noise, a loud yelp of pain as it slumped to the ground. Blood had clotted against the branch forming a bond that ripped apart as the dog fell. That and the collar had been all that had kept the exhausted animal upright. Fresh blood was now oozing from the wound.

The dog was free but it was clear to Tom it wasn't going anywhere soon, if ever. It lay flat out, the only thing moving were its eyes tracking the boy. Even those closed at times. Something had to be done or the animal would die.

The first thing to do was to stop the bleeding. Tom took out the wad of toilet paper he always carried when running in the forest. Unfolded, it formed a bandage wide enough to cover the wound. A red patch formed immediately and grew a little before the flow stopped.

"Okay," said Tom to himself. "Now I've got to go and get help." Then to the dog, "You okay with that? I won't be long. I'll bring a man who knows about dogs. He'll know what to do. His name's Dave Hughes." After a reassuring stroke of the head, he left.

Dave's door was open when Tom arrived. Before he had a chance to knock, Dave called out. "Come in, Tom. I was expecting you a little earlier."

"I got … caught … up," said Tom, still panting after the high-speed run out of the forest. "I found a dog … in the forest."

Dave looked up from the paper he was reading at the table. "And that's its collar you're holding, I gather? You'd better turn it off. There should be a switch alongside."

There was. Tom flicked it and the LED went out.

"Okay," said Dave, "now tell me about it."

Tom did, trying to get across the urgency of the situation. Dave remained sitting until the story had finished. Then he stood. "Right we'd better get back there. You get some water. There's an empty milk bottle in the sink. Fill that up. You should find a dog dish somewhere in the bottom cupboard. I'll get the first-aid kit." He took off into the bedroom.

Two minutes later they were in Dave's ute bouncing along the forestry track. Bouncing, but not rattling like Brandon's van did. This vehicle was designed for such surfaces, and was much newer. Watching Dave drive, Tom realised that, with other things on his mind, he hadn't noticed the stump that morning until now. It didn't seem to hinder Dave's driving. The only time he'd used it was to slip the transmission into drive when they'd started.

"That collar you're holding," said Dave. "It's a GPS tracking collar. I'm surprised the owner didn't track the dog when it didn't come back." He glanced over. "How long do you think it has been there?"

Tom pictured the scene in his head. The several piles of poo, the black, clotted blood, the skinny dog. "A long time," he said. "The thing's almost dead. Might be by the time we get there."

"Then there must be something wrong with the transmitter."

"Or maybe the hunter was injured too?" added Tom.

Dave looked across sharply. "Yes. That's a possibility," he said, grimly.

They travelled in silence after that, until they got to the turn around.

"Right, show me this dog," said Dave, taking the first aid kit out of the back. "Let's see what we can do for the poor creature."

Carrying the water and dish, Tom led the way into the grove of ferns. A surge of emotions gripped him when he saw the dog was still alive.

Dave knelt alongside, stroking the dog's head for a moment before testing the muscles of the hind legs.

"She's extremely dehydrated. That's probably her main problem. If we can get her to take water, then we can do something about that wound."

Tom poured some water into the dish and moved it close to the dog's snout. She moved her head trying to get a drink, but couldn't.

"Try lifting her front up," said Dave.

After several tries, Tom had her up enough to begin drinking.

"She's very light."

"Yes, she's been here a while all right. Maybe a week. If the hunter was injured somebody would have reported it by now. I think he just couldn't find her. I'll have a look at that transmitter when we get back. See if there's a name or something."

They watched her drink until she wanted a rest. Tom lay her back down so Dave could work on the wound.

The first-aid kit was designed for hunting-dog injuries. Most of the gear would work on a human, except for a few bandages designed to bind the body of a dog. After soaking the toilet paper off with water, Dave cleaned the wound with a dressing bandage.

"Fortunately, it's only the surface that's broken. There's nothing deep. There's no need to stitch her up. She should be right once she's rehydrated and had a feed."

Disinfectant powder was sprinkled on the wound, followed by a clean piece of dressing, which was bound in place around her body with a crepe bandage. Once it was clipped in place they were ready to leave.

"Can you carry her by yourself?" asked Dave, waggling his stump.

"Yeah, maybe. The problem is she's floppy."

"Okay, you hold her body with both hands, and I'll support her rear."

That worked, and soon they were lowering her onto the back of the ute.

"Do you think she might be the one that's been killing kiwis?" asked Tom.

"Not lately, she hasn't," replied Dave. "Before that, who knows." He thought for a bit. "Nah, I don't think it's her. I was reading in the paper this morning that they've found four others. One of them only a few days ago. I think she would have been hooked up at that stage."

He paused. "Look, you'd better ride in the back with her, in case she panics. You can do that?"

Tom answered by jumping onto the back, and sitting down beside the sick dog. "Yep, let's go."

Dave drove much slower on the way back giving Tom plenty of time to think, mostly about pig dogs and dead kiwis. He hoped Dave was right about this dog. He wanted her to recover. What would be the point of saving her if it turned out she was the killer? All of this would have been a big waste of time.

5

Buffy

First job back at Dave's house was to make the dog comfortable. Dave used an old duvet to make a bed in the corner of the lounge. After giving her another drink of water, she was lowered onto the bed.

"There you are Buffy," said Dave. "That should keep you comfy."

Tom looked at him. "How do you know her name is Buffy?"

"I don't. It's just habit. My bitch was called Buffy, sometimes Buff." He shrugged. "So that's what I'll call her until we find out her name. Which is what we can start doing now. You go out and get that GPS collar, while I get some tools."

When they were both seated at the table with everything they needed, Dave said, "My eyes aren't so good, so you'd better check for any names or anything. Look for scratches or writing with a vivid or something."

Picking up the collar, Tom could see lots of scratches, and while some did form a letter or two, the only one that looked intentional was the numeral '4'. This was alongside the manufacturer's name – *Acne Communications Company* – pressed into the plastic of the case. Below that was: *Made in the USA*. He showed it to Dave, who chuckled.

"I think it's meant to read Acme, not Acne," he said. "Made in the States, eh? That's not good."

"Why not?"

"Because they use the wrong frequency for New Zealand. The forestry industry use the same frequency so the public are banned from using it." He held up the collar. "If this was working in the forest it would interfere with the communications of logging gangs." He shook his head. "Not good. Not good at all. These were banned years back. The owner must know that."

"Would that be why he couldn't find her?"

"Yeah, I suppose it does work both ways. Let's pull it to bits and see if there's anything else that might stop it from working. It'll be easier if you take out the screws."

As soon as the last screw was removed, the plate popped off giving Tom a fright. "Whoa! There's lots of pressure in there."

"Wait!" ordered Dave. "Just hold it there for a moment." He got up and went to the kitchen, returning with a large metal roasting dish. "Okay. Gently put it in there."

"What's the problem?" asked Tom.

Dave picked up a screwdriver to use as a pointer. "See that there? That bulging part? That's where all the pressure is coming from. It's a lithium battery and it shouldn't be bulging like that. From now on we only touch it with pliers." He picked up a vice-grip tool. "I'll hold the box and you see if you can pull out the battery. Careful now."

This took some time because the battery was so swollen. It got even bigger as Tom eased it out. Eventually it sat in the dish, isolated from the collar, still growing in size.

"Now we'll stay back and let it settle," said Dave.

"What do you think will happen?"

"It might catch fire. That's not the original battery. See how some of the plastic has been scraped away from the bottom to make it fit. That's a cheapie bought off the Internet. Nobody should mess with—"

The sentence was never finished. One of the terminals had burst free of the battery, forced out by a spurt of flames. In less than a second the battery was a fireball, so hot Tom could feel it burning his face from more than a metre away. They moved further back.

"Wow, that's hot," said Tom.

Dave agreed. "Hope it doesn't set fire to my table top."

Slowly the inferno died until only the plastic was burning. Dave went outside to the ute, bringing back a fire extinguisher. One burst and the remaining flames died out. He then pushed the dish aside to examine the table top. While it hadn't caught fire, there was now a black, charred circle that wasn't there before.

"Imagine if we'd done this outside on the lawn," said Dave. "The whole forest would be alight by now."

Tom remained silent. He wasn't thinking of the forest. His mind was seeing the battery exploding in flames while the collar was still attached to Buffy. It was a terrible, frightening image.

Later that morning, Tom was by himself, sitting on the floor looking after Buffy while Dave was away in town getting dog food and some 'other things'.

Buffy was sleeping, her chest rising and lowering every five seconds or so. She looked to be doing well, not that he knew much about dogs. The family had not owned one, nor had he ever asked for one. And there certainly wasn't going to be one now, that was for sure. His mum wouldn't let any animal near her precious baby, and Brandon was never settled enough to own anything much.

"But if we *did* have one," Tom whispered to Buffy. "I would want it to be like you."

Yes, she was big enough to know you had a dog, not a cat or a squeaky toy. And her coat of grey with tan blotches made her interesting, especially the tan blob surrounding one eye. The only thing wrong with her was her shape. She was so skinny at the back. He could almost join his hands around the back of her body. Maybe she was part greyhound, or a racing dog of some sort. When she got better he'd have to test her out with a run.

These thoughts were interrupted by a vehicle pulling in. Sounded like Dave's ute. Then came a knock on the door, with a voice calling out.

"Anyone home?" A female, definitely not Dave.

Tom looked out the window to see a woman in a green blouse and shorts – a uniform. Which in Brandon's world meant she was from 'the authorities'. Tom could almost hear his father yelling, "Don't let her in."

"Yes," he called. "I'm coming."

After checking Buffy's bed couldn't be seen through the open door, he went outside.

"Hi," said the woman. "I'm Sally Page, from the Department of Conservation. I don't know if you've heard about it, but a number of kiwi have been attacked in this area recently."

Tom nodded.

"Well, saliva samples from the dead kiwi have been collected and will be DNA tested." She pulled a piece of paper out of her top pocket. "This is an order that allows me to take DNA samples from every dog in the area so we can look for a match."

Again Tom nodded.

"So, do you people own a dog?"

Tom's mind went into overdrive. *What to do? What to do?*

To gain time he said, "Actually this isn't my house. I'm being looked after by Dave."

"Okay, does Dave own a dog?"

Then it came to him. Just answer the question.

"No, Dave doesn't own one."

"What about you? Are you from that other place?" She pointed towards Brandon's hut. "There was nobody home there."

"Yeah, that's our place. We don't own one either."

"Okay … um …" Then she made up her mind, bringing out a card. "Right, if you do see a dog loose in the area, contact me immediately." She handed over the card. "Can you do that?"

"Ah … yeah …," mumbled Tom, his mind elsewhere. Already he was feeling guilty. He wanted to help but didn't know how much he should tell. What would Dave want him to do?

Sally saw his indecision. "You got something you want to tell me?"

"We found one of those dead kiwis, you know. I told a man called Mike. He said he'd pass on the information. Did he do that?"

Sally's face brightened. "Ah, you must be Tom, the boy who caught the pig." Then she frowned. "You should not have let that sow loose in the forest," she said, sternly.

"That's what Mike told me to do."

Her eyes rolled. "Yes, he would, wouldn't he. Mike Davidson doesn't always get things right. He only looks after himself, that man."

Tom shrugged, not knowing what she was talking about.

"Mike's a pig hunter," she explained. "He wanted that young sow returned so she could breed. That's not good for the kiwi. Your actions will put more pigs in the forest when already there's more than enough."

That helped make up Tom's mind. He'd been about to tell her about Buffy. But why should he, if she was going to be grumpy? He remained silent and shortly afterwards she left.

One of the 'other things' that Dave returned with was a microchip scanner he'd borrowed from a friend.

"We need to find the owner of this dog, if we can."

Tom agreed even though it wasn't what he wanted. Already he was thinking of Buffy as his own dog.

"Okay, girl," said Dave moving the machine towards

Buffy. "This won't hurt at all."

She lifted her head, to take in what was happening.

"That's good. You're coming right aren't you?"

He started with her shoulder and moved down the back, across the left thigh, and back up to the shoulders. No sounds came from the machine.

"All right we need to do the other side. If you can lift her up and hold her, I'll do the rest."

That was done, and still there was no response from the machine.

"She's not chipped," Dave declared.

"What does that mean?"

"Well, she hasn't been registered, which means we can't find out who owns her that way."

"Would they put her in a pound if she was discovered?"

"Yes, if the dog officer caught her."

"What about the Department of Conservation?"

"DoC? Why do you mention them?"

Tom told him of the visitor.

"You did the right thing," said Dave when the story was finished. "And yes, they would have taken her away, and we don't want that."

"You want to keep her?" asked Tom, hopefully.

"No, we need to find the owner so we can take the batteries out of the rest of those collars. Did you see the number four scratched on that one?"

"Yeah."

"That means there's at least three more of them. He could even use more than four dogs."

"Do you think the others might catch fire too?"

"They might. Even if they don't, every time he uses them they're messing up communications in the forest. For that reason alone they need to be taken out of service."

"So how will we find him?"

Dave pointed to Buffy. "We won't. She will. She knows where he lives. In a few days when she's better she'll show us where. Even if we have to drive over half of Northland, we have a duty to find her owner."

They sat for a while beside Buffy, thinking.

"You know, Tom, lots of people call pig dogs mongrels. Most of the time that's not true. Buffy's no mongrel, but chances are when we find her owner we'll meet somebody who is."

6

Harvey

As Tom expected, Brandon arrived well after five o'clock that evening, although this time he hadn't minded waiting around. They'd fed Buffy at lunchtime, and again at four o'clock. Both times Tom had needed to support her as she still couldn't stand. Then, while he was sitting beside her waiting for Brandon, she staggered to her feet, and turned two circles before flopping down in a more comfortable position.

"Yesss," he whispered, stroking her head. "You're getting much better, aren't you? Soon you'll be able to come running with me."

When Brandon did turn up he seemed happier than usual, as if he'd had a pay rise or something. He even crouched down to stroke Buffy, while he listened to Tom's account of the day's events as if he was truly interested.

Afterwards he told Tom to go home ahead of him while he had a chat to Dave about something.

Tom had to wait until after dinner before he was let into the secret. When the TV programme they were watching finished, Brandon picked up the remote and muted the sound.

"We need to have a discussion," he said.

"Yeah, okay."

"I've got a date tomorrow night."

That made Tom take more interest. "What sort of date? A *date* date?"

Brandon gave a stupid grin. "Yeah."

"Who with?"

"You've met her."

"When?"

"Recently. End of last week."

Tom thought back. The only new woman he'd met was … "That reporter? Marika somebody?"

"Yeah, Marika Greenwell." Brandon was still grinning.

"But … but … you were shouting at each other."

Brandon shrugged. "Sometimes it happens like that. At least she noticed me. Enough to come up and talk to me after work today. So I asked her out to dinner, and she said yes."

This was all too new for Tom. While his mother had found another partner and even had a baby, he'd not expected his father to be looking for someone. He asked, "Does that mean you've decided to stay in Kerikeri?"

"Aw, it's a bit early to say that. When the picking season finishes I don't know what I'll be doing."

This was the chance Tom had been waiting for. "Dad, I like it here," he began. "This school's the best I've been to. I want to stay here. They've got a great sports programme. And there's some triathlons I want to enter later in the year, but I've got to let them know when school goes back."

Brandon was shaking his head. "You can't make that sort of commitment, Tom. Your mum still has the final say. If she wants you back, there's nothing I can do to stop it."

"She'd be okay if we stayed in one place."

"She might be and then she might not be."

Tom thought of saying more, before deciding against it. If he went on they'd end up having an argument. He returned to the original topic.

"So, you've got a date tomorrow night. What happens to me?"

"Dave's agreed to feed you dinner and put you up for the night. He says you can sleep on the sofa."

Tom almost cheered. That was the answer he'd wanted, because the sofa was right beside Buffy.

Next morning, Tom went over to Dave's straight after breakfast, keen to see how Buffy was getting on.

"She's much better," said Dave when Tom walked in the door. "I think we should take the bandage off and see if she can do without it."

Buffy managed to support herself while the crepe bandage was unwound. She cringed a little when the gauze was first touched, but allowed Dave to soak it off without complaint. The wound looked pink and healthy.

"I'll give it another dusting with antiseptic, but leave it uncovered. It'll heal up quicker that way." As he was doing that he asked, "What have you got in mind for today?"

"A bike ride," replied Tom without hesitation.

"In the forest?"

"No. I need to do some training on sealed roads. I thought I'd go to the end of Inlet Road. Can I get down to the sea there?"

"You'd need to turn onto Wharau Road. That gets you down to the mouth of the inlet. You planning to have a swim?"

"Yeah." Tom told him about his hopes to compete in the triathlon.

"Won't the water be a bit cold from now on?" asked Dave.

"The competition's not until the end of the year. If I get

52

into the team we'll have two sessions a week in the heated pool at Kawakawa. I thought I'd get a head start."

After making some lunch and saying goodbye to Buffy, Tom was on his way.

At the intersection of their track with Inlet Road he had to wait for a stream of traffic to pass before making a right turn. This gave him a chance to study the entrance to the subdivision opposite. A man standing on scaffolding with his back to him, was laying the top row of blocks onto a high wall, the last part of a fence that enclosed the whole subdivision. The people who lived there, clearly liked privacy.

When a gap in the traffic came, Tom accelerated across the road. At the same time a dog rushed out through the gate barking. A black Labrador.

"Get out of it!" yelled Tom, kicking out his leg, turning the wheel sharply.

Unfortunately the entranceway hadn't been sealed and the bike skidded causing Tom to fall. The dog stood over him, barking loudly into his face.

"Get off! Get off!" screamed Tom.

Then came another voice louder and deeper. "Harvey! Get back!" This came from the block-layer.

The dog stopped barking, but didn't back away.

"Get out of it Harvey!" yelled the block-layer.

This time the dog obeyed, slinking off behind the wall.

"You should keep your dog under better control," said Tom, brushing himself off and climbing to his feet. "I could have got run over."

"He's not my dog, Tom."

Tom looked up to see who knew his name. It was Mike Davidson again.

"So, whose is it?"

"Mrs Hopwood's. She's the developer of this place. Owns that big house down the end there. Climb up here and have a look."

From the top of the scaffold, Tom could see the extent of the subdivision. There were nine houses altogether. Six still had builders all over them, only one was fully completed. That was the one Mike was indicating, a two-storey mansion.

"The dog was her husband's, but he died. She's taken over both the subdivision and the dog. She can't control either properly. As far as I'm concerned the dog should be shot. It's nothing but trouble. Thing never wears a collar. It's always outside the gate. A couple of mornings I've seen it come back across the road from the forest. Makes me suspicious that does, what with all these kiwis being killed. I've already reported it to DoC."

The dog began barking again, this time in a friendly, excited way.

"Uh oh," said Mike. "Here comes the witch." The

54

dog was bounding towards a woman walking down the driveway. She didn't look like a witch to Tom. In fact she looked quite pleasant in her colourful summer clothing.

"She's seen what happened on the security camera," continued Mike, pointing to a black box high on a post not far inside the gate. "She'll be all apologetic. Say it won't happen again. But it will." He gave a snort. "Look at the dog, will you? Making out it's the perfect pet. He's got her sorted."

Harvey was trotting obediently beside Mrs Hopwood, as if he was completely under her control.

"Are you all right?" she asked.

"Yeah, nothing broken," said Tom.

"I'm sorry about that. He sneaks out of the house when I'm not looking. And I can't close all the doors, it's so hot."

"Maybe you need a fence around *your* house," said Tom.

She spread her arms wide. "The only fence we're having is this one. It will do the job for all the residents." She turned and glared at Mike. "That's if it ever gets finished. It seems to be taking forever."

Mike mumbled something under his breath.

"What was that?" she said, sharply. Now she sounded like a witch.

"I said it will be finished this week," said Mike with a sigh. "That's if you don't change the plans again."

She turned on him. "The plans only change because you say you can't do things. Things other block-layers seem to be quite capable of doing."

She swivelled around and marched back up the drive. When the dog didn't follow straight away, she turned and called him. "Come on Harvey. Get back inside."

Harvey lowered his head and followed.

Mike mumbled again. It sounded like 'witch', but it wasn't quite that.

There was no missing the fact that the road to the end of the inlet passed through kiwi country. There were several signs warning drivers to beware of kiwis at night. In places white outlines of the birds were painted on the road. One sign had a photo of a dead kiwi looking much like the one Tom had seen in the forest, except this one had been killed by a car, not a dog. Waitangi Forest lined the right side of the road, farmland and lifestyle blocks filled the left. Many of the fences were made of scoria, suggesting there had once been a volcano nearby.

Although the road was narrow in places, Tom was able to set a good pace as all the traffic was heading the other way, into town. Side roads led off to the inlet where Tom could see beach houses, some of them as big as Mrs Hopwood's mansion.

The forest was replaced by scrubland at the Wharau

Road turnoff. From there on he had the road to himself and he forced out the last four kilometres as hard as he could. When he got to the beach, he threw his bike to the ground, stripped down to his shorts and dived into the sea, whooping with shock and joy at the coldness of the water.

Later, he sat on the tiny beach, drying in the sun, thinking how good life was. He was happier than he could remember. Being looked after by Dave Hughes was much better than he'd anticipated. His dad was showing signs of settling down. And, with any luck, he'd soon have a dog to keep him company. Everything was looking great.

On the return journey, mid-afternoon, he took a side road heading south which he thought might link up with the tracks in the forest. The seal ended after a hundred metres which was promising as all the forestry tracks were unsealed. The land on the left was still being farmed, but that on the right, closer to the forest, was quickly turning into wasteland. A few cattle were forcing their way through gorse searching for any remaining pasture.

Not far beyond was a house looking as neglected as the land around it. Past that the road came to a gate. Even though the road continued much the same as before, the gate was locked with a hand-painted board alongside saying:

KEEP OUT

PRIVATE PROPERTY

Tom could see in the distance that the road did go into the forest. He was tempted to lift his bike over the gate and keep going. But then dogs began barking from behind the house, loud and angry enough to put off any trespasser. He turned around.

Passing the house again, he noted the name on the letterbox was M J Davidson. Could that be Mike Davidson? The DoC lady had said Mike was a pig hunter. Maybe those were his dogs out the back. Then another thought came into his head. Had the DoC lady collected DNA samples from this far out? If not, then she should have. While it was a long way around by road, a shortcut through the forest would make it fairly close to where the dead kiwis had been found.

7

Logging Gang

Dinner that Tuesday night was different to normal for Tom. Dave had lived by himself most of his life and had become a pretty good cook. The main dish was spinach and leek filo, two vegetables Tom usually hated. But the way Dave combined them with egg, cheese and bacon bits, turned them into a delicious meal. Much better than he would have got, if Brandon had cooked.

After discussing Tom's day, Dave led the conversation around to Buffy.

"We've got to have her DNA tested," he said.

Tom looked up, shocked. "Why? Do you think she's the kiwi killer?"

"No, I don't. But we can't ignore that it *is* a possibility."

Tom shook his head violently. "No! She wouldn't do that."

"Tom! Just hold on. Hear me out." When Tom had calmed a little, Dave went on. "I have no idea how long you'll be in this town, but I've been here for a long time already, and I plan to be here a lot longer. Imagine what would happen if it became known that I'd hidden a dog that could be a kiwi killer. I'd lose my friends and any standing I have in this community. Sooner or later I'd have to leave."

"What are you going to do?" asked Tom, sulkily. "Ring the authorities?" He spat the words out.

"No. We've discussed that before. They're sure to take her away and we don't want that. I think we should tell Marika Greenwell. Use her as a go-between."

"The reporter?" shouted Tom. "She'll tell everybody."

Dave shook his head. "I don't think so. Because we've got an even better story for her. Buffy's story. If we tell Marika about the illegal collars and the batteries, I'm sure she'll want to know more. She might even help us find the owner. Then she can tell the story."

"But what if the test says Buffy is a killer?" asked Tom.

"Then we'll have to live with that. As far as Marika is concerned that would just add to the story."

After a bit more discussion they agreed on a plan of action. In the morning Brandon would be asked to pass a message to Marika. If she accepted certain terms, then she'd be told where to come. They'd then sort the rest out face to face.

Next morning, when Brandon hadn't arrived at Dave's by eight o'clock, Tom went over to see if he'd made it home. He had, but was sleeping in. Even when he finally arrived at Dave's house, he still seemed to be in a bit of a dream. Dave had to explain a couple of times what they wanted him to do. He agreed, but instead of phoning in front of the others, he went outside to make the call. Five minutes later he came in saying Marika would be over soon. Then he left for work.

'Soon' was certainly that. She must have passed Brandon almost before he got off the track.

After Tom introduced her to Dave, they got down to business. The result was: yes, Marika wanted the story, and yes, she would hold it until they had tried to find the owner.

"But if the DNA result comes out positive for Buffy, I'll publish right away. That's not something I can hold back."

Tom and Dave agreed to that.

"You realise that most likely she'll be put down if it is her?"

"Couldn't she be trained not to go near kiwis?" asked Tom.

"Aversion training?" said Marika. "That doesn't always work, not if a dog has killed before."

"But it might work, mightn't it?"

"Yes, it could be tried." She studied him for a moment.

"You've become attached to her, haven't you?"

"Yes. I want her to be my dog."

"Have you talked to Brandon about this?"

"Hold it there," interrupted Dave. "Before we do anything more, let's sort out some other stuff. Have any more kiwis been reported dead in the last few days?"

"You mean since you found the dog?"

Dave nodded.

"Unfortunately, no. So she's not off the hook, I'm sorry to say."

"Okay then," said Dave. "Let's take these samples. Do you know what to do?"

Marika did. She'd written a story about it during earlier kiwi attacks. A few hairs had to be extracted and a sample of skin removed. Buffy didn't object to a bit of skin being trimmed from around the wound, but she did yelp when some hairs were pulled out. Both samples were put in zippered plastic bags. It would take four or five days before the results would be known.

"She's a nice dog," said Marika, standing by her vehicle preparing to leave. "I sure hope she's not the killer. But if she is, it would be best if we found the real owner so you don't get charged. Anyone who is responsible for a dog that kills protected wildlife can be fined $20,000 or even jailed. I don't want that to happen to you." With that, she drove off.

Later that morning, Buffy and her bed were loaded into the front of the ute. They were off to visit Dave's old logging gang. If anyone knew what was going on in Waitangi Forest, the logging workers would.

Dave wore his old gear: high-visibility jacket, steel-capped boots, and a helmet with a fold-down visor. Tom had pulled on his hi-vis cycling vest. They were hoping to pick up the rest of the gear he'd need at the site.

At the entrance to the forest track, Dave turned on the ute's headlights, something Tom had also noticed on the trip in to save Buffy. "Why the lights?" he asked.

"It's the rule. All vehicles in a working forest must have headlights on. It helps the truck drivers see what's coming. We're the intruders here. The forestry gangs all know where their own vehicles are because they're in radio communication. They have strict rules about movements. That can all be stuffed up by other vehicles like us."

Tom thought about this. "Or if the radios don't work," he added.

"Dead right," said Dave. "That's why we need to find out who's using those American transmitters. Confiscate them before they start causing problems."

The working site was a long way into the forest, closer to the Waitangi side than Kerikeri. Dave had timed their visit so they arrived at break time, otherwise they wouldn't have been allowed past the security man at the entranceway. Even then, they had to report to the site office and get Tom fitted with a hardhat and toe guards before going further.

The workers were sitting around on logs, each with a thermos and a bag of food alongside. As soon as Dave arrived he became the centre of attention. Everyone wanted to shake his hand and find out how he was getting on. Several told jokes about people with missing limbs. Tom liked the one that involved a hitchhiker: A man stops his car to check whether it's safe to pick up a hitchhiker or not, and sees that he's got only one arm. "Ah," he says. "You look pretty 'armless . 'Op in."

Most of the other jokes were not repeatable.

After ten minutes, Dave finally got a chance to ask his questions.

"You seen any dogs in the forest recently?"

"Seen a few," said Norm, a guy Tom recognised as the other hunter in the photo on Dave's wall. "You don't ever get a good look at them though."

"I think you'd notice this one," said Dave. "Go and get her Tom."

Tom brought Buffy out of the ute and let her walk around the seated workers. Although she moved stiffly,

64

she was alert enough to show an interest in the food.

"Nice looking dog," said Norm. "What's her story?"

Dave filled them in and then asked. "Anybody seen her before, or know who owns her?"

"I've not seen her," said a man who seemed to be the foreman. "But that collar you said she was wearing must be what's been messing with the radios. We've had problems for weeks now. I've reported it to head office. They were going to take it to the police. Imagine if the radios had been down when you had your accident, Dave. You would have lost more than your arm, you would have lost your life."

There was much nodding at this.

"Yeah," said Dave, "that's why we want to get this sorted."

"Have you checked with the pig hunting club?" asked one.

"Not yet. But I doubt any club member would use illegal collars."

"No, they wouldn't," said Norm. "This hunter's a rogue." He then nodded towards Buffy. "Might be worth driving around some of the roads. If she picks up the scent of the others in the pack, she'd soon tell you."

"That's what we're going to try next," said Dave. "Um … could you all … um … keep quiet about her. She's not chipped and if they take her away, it'll make it harder to find the guy."

"Sure," said the foreman, standing. "You find this guy and then let us know. We'll take it to the police. We need to get those transmitters out of action before something goes terribly wrong."

Work resumed, with Dave and Tom allowed to watch as long as they stayed close to the site office. While there was no chance of talking above the noise, Tom could see how it worked. Basically, the trees were felled by chainsaws, before huge machines took over, dragging, lifting, stripping, and trimming the logs as if they were no more than sticks. Communication was by coded beeps from air horns. It all seemed under control, but Tom could see it only needed one thing to get out of sequence and everything could go wrong. No wonder workers lost limbs and some their lives.

On the way home, Buffy sat on her bed looking out the windscreen, taking in her surroundings. Maybe she recognised where they were, maybe she didn't. While she watched the forest, Tom watched her, thrilled she was looking so good. Secretly, he was also pleased that none of the loggers had identified her. He was in two minds about finding the owner. Yes, he knew it was important to get the transmitters out of action, but if the man was such a rogue, then he didn't deserve to get Buffy back. She needed an owner who would love her, somebody like—

Buffy made them both jump with a sudden bark, deafeningly loud in the confines of the cab.

"Stop it!" shouted Dave and Tom together.

She was standing, staring at the undergrowth on the left.

Dave slowed the ute. "She's seen something."

A black shape could be seen running through the undergrowth.

"Is that the pig you caught?" asked Dave.

Then the animal sprinted through a gap in the ferns.

"No, it's not," said Tom. "That's a dog."

Buffy resumed barking, her nose touching the windscreen.

"I think she recognises it," said Dave. "Didn't look much like a pig dog, but. More like a Labrador. Let's see if it will come to us." He stopped, climbed out, put his fingers to his mouth and gave a piercing whistle.

Tom held onto Buffy to stop her jumping out too. The barking changed to a whine.

Another whistle.

"No," said Dave, climbing back in. "It's taken off."

Buffy settled and they resumed their journey.

"That was somebody's pet," said Dave after a while. "I hope that one's had its DNA taken. Seems mighty suspicious to me, the way it ran off." He turned to Tom. "Did you see if it had a collar on or not?"

"There was no collar," said Tom, quietly. He could have added, "Just like Mrs Hopwood's dog, Harvey." Instead, he let it be.

8

Crash

Thursday morning Tom got up at six o'clock when Brandon's alarm went off. He wanted to do a time trial along Inlet Road before the traffic built up. This would be a benchmark time for future training.

The track to the road was always dim because of overhanging trees. At that time on an April morning it was pretty much dark – the ideal hiding place for a black dog.

Tom heard the snarl and saw the white teeth at the same time. Then it was lunging at him, smashing into the front wheel. The bike toppled sideways. Tom thrust up with his legs, arms out, hoping to cushion the fall. The dog yelped. The bike crashed. Tom fell. And when it was all over, he was lying in the long grass at the edge of the track, with the dog standing over him, tongue out, panting, as if waiting for a reward.

"Harvey!" shouted Tom. "Why do you do that?"

More panting.

Tom sighed. "Get back so I can get up."

Still more panting.

In the end Tom had to push the dog sideways so he could climb to his feet. He tested his legs and arms. Nothing seemed damaged. The same couldn't be said for the bike though. Three broken spokes stuck out from the front hub.

Tom leant the bike against a tree and threaded the broken spokes through others so the bike could be wheeled back home. Riding it would only cause more damage to the wheel. The repair was already going to cost more money than Tom had.

Meanwhile, Harvey sat on the track watching Tom at work, seemingly pleased with himself.

Tom turned on him. "Look what you've done, you stupid mutt. That's going to cost me heaps. Why don't you stay inside the gate?"

Now Harvey realised he was in trouble. He crouched down until his nose was on the ground, his sad eyes looking up at the angry boy.

"Oh Harvey," sighed Tom. "We'd better get you back home." He'd started to walk towards the road when he had another thought. He returned to the bike. "I'm taking this with us. Your owner needs to see this damage. Come on Harvey, let's go."

The front door to Mrs Hopwood's mansion was wide open. Harvey walked straight in, giving the impression the door was always open for him.

Tom propped his bike against a pillar before ringing the doorbell and waiting.

Harvey returned with his owner.

Mrs Hopwood saw who it was and sighed. "Okay, what was it this time?"

"He lunged at me again," said Tom. "Damaged my bike."

"I'll pay," she said, without pause. "How much?"

"I won't know until I take it into the bike shop."

"All right. I know the owner. I'll give him a call and he can charge me back." Another sigh. "You'd better come in so I can write down your name and details."

They went into a kitchen gleaming with stainless steel appliances. Tom was invited to sit on a stool at a polished-stone breakfast bar.

"You had breakfast?"

"No. I'll have it when I get home."

"How about sausage and egg?"

Tom smiled. "Yeah, all right."

As she cooked, she quizzed him about where he lived, who else was in the family, what school he went to, where his father worked – the full interrogation. Tom answered honestly without going into detail about why the family didn't live together. Her little nods indicated she was quite capable of filling in the gaps.

When breakfast was served, she joined him at the bar. Harvey moved until he was crouched beside Tom's stool, as if waiting for something.

"He's hoping to get your plate to clean up."

"Do you let him do that?"

"Yes." Her eyes twinkled. "I call it the pre-rinse before it goes in the dishwasher. Saves on water."

Tom chuckled. "He's a nice dog."

"Yes. He was mainly my husband's. When he died I wasn't sure I wanted a dog, but now I've become very attached to Harvey. He's great company." The eyes twinkled again. "Never argues about a thing."

This was Tom's chance.

"Except going out the gate," he said, staring her in the eyes. "Harvey was on the other side of the road when he attacked my bike. He was in the forest."

She turned away. "Yes, that worries me. The problem is we can't have a gate put on until that man finishes the fence."

"You could tie him up."

"But he's never been tied up in his life. That would be unfair."

"It'll be worse if the authorities find him near the kiwis.

We saw a dog that looked like him well away from the road yesterday."

Mrs Hopwood took in a deep breath, exhaling slowly.

Tom pushed on. "He could be the kiwi killer."

"No!" she cried. "No! Harvey would never do that."

"How would you know? Has he had aversion training?"

She shook her head. "The DoC people came and took samples, though. Surely they would have got back to me if he's involved."

"I don't think the results are known yet," said Tom.

He was about to push more when he saw tears in her eyes. Instead he asked, "Mrs Hopwood, have you got a collar?"

She nodded.

"Then put it on him and keep him shut in the house."

"Yes," she said. "I'll do that." Then she gave a crooked smile. "And thank you young man for reminding an old lady of her responsibilities."

Tom also smiled, sensing they had just become friends.

Tom and Dave went into town after lunch, with Buffy in the cab, and the bike on the back.

Dave went to the supermarket while Tom sorted things out in the bike shop. Mrs Hopwood had kept her word and rung to arrange payment. She'd also suggested Tom could choose something extra to have fitted if he wanted. After much discussion Tom chose a speed and distance computer that would help with his training. The job would be finished by closing time at five o'clock, leaving four hours to search for Buffy's owner.

With no idea of where the pig hunter might live, they decided to do a grid search of Kerikeri. While Buffy took plenty of interest in where they went, nothing caused her to get excited. She did react to any dogs they saw, but none of them caused her to bark like she had in the forest.

After covering the streets around the town, they moved out to the rural roads where there were lots of lifestyle blocks, on roads Tom hadn't known existed. And yet there was still no major reaction from Buffy.

At quarter to five, Dave decided to quit and head back to town.

"This is stupid," he said. "The hunter could have come from miles away. Nothing says he's from Kerikeri. He could be anywhere up north. Kawakawa, Kaikohe, he could even have come down from Kaitaia."

Tom said nothing. He had an idea where to search next, but it could wait until after they'd picked up the bike.

Once the bike was on the back they set off for home. As they approached the bridge over the mangroves Tom said, "Don't turn off. Keep going. There's something I want to check out."

As they went past the new subdivision, Tom noted that another row of blocks had been added. It did look as if Mike Davidson would finish before the week was out as he had promised.

The man himself was not there, but a couple of new temporary posts had been put in beside the concrete ones. Tied to them with rope was a wire farm gate. Tom nodded to himself: Mrs Hopwood had taken their conversation seriously.

"How far do you want me to go?" asked Dave.

"Keep going until we're past the forest."

"What are we looking for?"

"A place where I heard a lot of dogs the other day."

"Okay. Tell me when we get there."

Buffy showed increasing interest as they travelled further along Inlet Road.

"You need to turn right soon," said Tom, now almost as excited as Buffy.

"Onto Bush Road?" asked Dave.

"I don't know what it's called. It's a gravel road that leads to the forest."

"Yeah, I know it," said Dave. Then after they'd made the turn, he added, "Seems like Buffy does too."

She was breathing quickly, her mouth open, her eyes bright, peering forward, anticipating what would appear soon.

Only when the house came into view, did she start barking, climbing onto Dave's lap to get her head out the side window.

"Get off, Buffy," growled Dave. "I get the message. That's your home."

Tom put his arms around her, pulling her back.

"Thanks," said Dave. "I'm going to drive past."

"There's a locked gate up here a bit," said Tom.

"I'll stop and turn around there. We need to do a bit of thinking."

Buffy had stopped barking when they got to the gate, but the dogs behind the house hadn't. It sounded like there was a pack of them.

After the ute had been turned, they sat studying the house expecting something to happen. Buffy was back sitting in the middle, staring at the house more intensely than either human. She knew somebody would come out soon.

When a man did appear out a side door, he first looked across to the ute, pausing a moment, before heading around the back to yell at the dogs.

"That's Mike Davidson," said Tom.

"Oh yeah? How come you know that?"

Tom explained.

"Mmm, I've heard of him," said Dave. "Can't say I've ever met him."

"What are we going to do?"

"Wait a while and see what happens."

First, the dogs quietened. Then Davidson reappeared to stare long and hard at the ute.

Buffy let out a little growl.

For a time it looked as if Davidson might come over. In the end he turned and went back inside.

"You going to take her back?" asked Tom, quietly.

Dave shook his head. "Nope. I know she wants to be with her pack, but I don't think that's the best thing for her."

"So what do we do?"

"What we do," said Dave, "is take her back home and hold her until she's fully recovered. In the meantime I'm going to ask around about this Mike Davidson. Find out everything we can. I want to be prepared before we come back. He's not going to like what we're going to say." He paused. "We need to be careful, because things could get ugly very, very quickly."

9

Calm before the Storm

Friday morning Tom took Buffy on their first walk together. Her wound had healed enough to use a collar padded with cloth.

The collar and lead had come from Dave's store of dog gear previously used by the original Buffy. Even though the registration tag was years out of date and the wrong colour, they left it there thinking it was better than nothing. Not that Tom intended going out on the road where people would see them. He planned to stick to the quiet of the forest.

Before he left, Dave warned him that most pig dogs weren't taken for walks. Their only job was to chase and bail up a pig. She might not know what was expected of her on a walk.

This was confirmed over the first hundred metres where it became very clear Buffy was not used to being on a lead.

She kept diving sideways to sniff things, almost pulling Tom's arm out of the socket, and hurting herself at the same time.

"Take it easy, Buffy," growled Tom. "Walk quietly."

She lowered her head and walked alongside, although obviously not enjoying the experience. This worked for a minute or so before something especially smelly grabbed her attention, and she was back to tugging sideways.

Tom sat her down. "What will you do if I let you off? Will you behave yourself?"

Buffy wagged her tail.

"You won't run away?"

More wagging.

Tom had trouble removing the clip from the collar, his hand was shaking so much. This experiment could go horribly wrong. What if she wouldn't come when called? What if she decided to find her way home? What if she caught the scent of a pig or, worse still, sniffed out a kiwi burrow?

None of that happened. After the lead had been removed she stayed sitting, waiting to be released.

Tom gave the nod. "Okay, Buffy."

Instead of rushing off, she stayed alongside Tom for a time, as if proving she could be trusted. Eventually, a smell took her sideways. Tom kept walking, hoping she'd catch up soon. Which she did, moving past him on to the next smell, whatever it was. And that was how the rest of the walk went: Tom walking steadily, Buffy stop-starting.

Not wanting to tire her too much, he turned back after a kilometre, returning to Dave's place half an hour after they'd left. Before going inside, Tom sat her down and gave her a thank you pat. He was now more determined than ever to keep this dog as his own.

Later on Dave took them back to the logging site with the intention of asking his mates about Mike Davidson.

They were met by the foreman in the site office.

"Ah, Dave, Norm said you were coming for smoko, very timely. You know Ray, our security man?"

Dave nodded, they'd spoken to him on the way into the site.

"He's heading off tonight to Auckland. His mum's in hospital. He'll be back Monday. The trouble is we've now got to work on Sunday."

"Sunday? That's unusual," said Dave.

"Yeah. It's because of this hurricane that's coming. Cyclone Pene. Have you heard about it?"

"No. Nothing."

"Well, it's been moving down from the tropics for a few days now. Hasn't caused any damage so far, but the remnants are expected to hit us late Monday, early Tuesday. If we don't get the rest of this block on the ground before then, the storm will do it for us." He let out a sigh. "Then we'd have a heck of a mess to clean up. Lose half the timber as well. The bosses don't want that. So we're working Sunday."

"And you want me to do security?"

"Yeah. You know what's involved. Just keeping the book of who comes in and goes out. Make sure there's not too many trucks up top at the same time. That sort of thing."

Dave looked at Tom. "Your dad working Sunday?"

Tom shrugged. "I don't know. He never tells me things like that. Anyway, I can look after myself and Buffy."

Dave turned back to the foreman. "Yeah, I can do it. What time you starting?"

"Usual time, six o'clock. But we'll be working later. The boys have agreed to go through till five. Ten hours will get most of it done. We should be able to clean up the rest Monday morning."

After that they joined the workers sitting on the logs. All the talk was about the coming storm and what it would do to the trees. The problem was that during the felling of a block, lots of trees were exposed that had never experienced the wind: they'd always been sheltered by those around the outside. That was the case with this block.

Tom could see what they were talking about. The trees nearby had bare trunks reaching high into the sky with a Christmas-tree of green at the very top. Even to him it looked like if you pushed one, they'd all fall over. The solution was to fell them in an orderly way before the storm came.

Not until they were about to return to work was Dave able to ask about Mike Davidson. Most of them knew of him, without being close.

"Arrived here a couple of years ago," said one. "Bought that property down Bush Road. Does a bit of pig hunting, both with dogs and shooting."

"I've met him a couple of times," added another. "Talks about shooting things a lot. Could be all talk."

"I know he's had a few run-ins over jobs he's done," said Norm. "Slow to complete them and then lots of stuff needs fixing." He pointed to Buffy who was sitting at Tom's feet. "Why you asking? Is she one of his?"

"It's a possibility."

"Go to the police, mate," said Norm. "Using those transmitters is a criminal matter. Let them sort it out."

"Aw, I don't want to put a guy crook with the police. Not without giving him a chance to sort it out for himself."

Norm shook his head. "You're far too fair, Dave. From what I've heard about Mike Davidson he's not the type to be told what to do. You take care, mate. And if you need any help, give us a call."

Around five o'clock that afternoon Marika Greenwell arrived at Brandon and Tom's place.

Tom was playing with Buffy on the lawn outside Dave's when he heard the vehicle pull up. The engine sounded much too smooth to be Brandon's van, so he led Buffy along the path to check it out.

"Hello Tom," said Marika. "Bran not home yet?"

So it's 'Bran' already, thought Tom. That was what his mum used to call him, now she used Brandon.

Out loud he said, "Nah. You're a bit early for him. He could be hours yet."

"He said he'd be home and ready by five. We're going out for the evening."

This was news to Tom.

"I guess he's running a bit late," Marika added.

"He's always late," complained Tom. "Get used to it."

Marika raised her eyebrows, but said nothing.

"Look," he said, "why don't you come over to Dave's, we'll hear Dad arrive from there."

Dave was sitting in a chair on the lawn enjoying the late-afternoon sun. After greetings, Marika asked, "So how's our story about the transmitters going. When am I going to be able to publish? Our deadline for Thursday's edition is Wednesday midday."

"We're getting there," said Dave. "We have a suspect."

"Who?"

Dave took his time before answering. "Mike Davidson."

Tom expected Marika to show surprise. Instead she gave a little nod.

"You expected that?" asked Dave.

"Let's just say, I'm not surprised he'd be doing something illegal. He has a history."

"Tell us."

"Mike lived in Dargaville before he came up here a couple of years back. He had a property out of town, much like that one on Bush Road. One day a man came onto the place and Mike confronted him with a shotgun, telling him to leave. The man wouldn't, so Mike fired off a couple of cartridges. They weren't fired at the man but, wisely, he took off before some were. He went straight to the police and laid a complaint. It turned out the man was on a designated road that has never been built. It's public land, a so-called paper road. Mike had access to it because it was next to his place. The police charged Mike with reckless discharge of a firearm. That's $4,000 or three years prison, right there."

She paused and took a few deep breaths before continuing. "In the end he got nothing. When it came to court it was revealed the man was an activist who set out to draw attention to public land being used privately. It was considered he provoked the reaction. In the end, the judge gave Mike a telling off, before discharging him without

84

conviction as long as he did some community work. I don't know what that was, but I gather he completed it because I've seen nothing in court documents since. The thing is, Dave, I think you need to be careful in dealing with Mike Davidson. What have you got against him so far?"

Dave outlined Buffy's reaction to their drive along Bush Road.

"So he's got a lot of dogs there?" said Marika. "That's interesting. I wonder if they were tested by DoC. That road doubles back onto the forest. It wouldn't be far from there to where most of the dead kiwi were found."

"You think he's harbouring a kiwi killer as well?" asked Dave.

Marika shrugged. "I honestly don't know. Probably not. It's just that he's very vocal about kiwi killers. Who knows?"

"When will the results be through?" asked Dave.

"Monday, I believe." She looked down to Buffy. "You know if it is her, then I'll publish anyway, even if we haven't confirmed the owner."

Before Dave could answer they heard the unmistakeable sound of Brandon's van arriving home.

Marika looked at her watch, then at Tom. "You said he'd be hours late. It's only twenty minutes."

"Must be because it's you," mumbled Tom.

She was about to take off down the path when she turned back. "When are you visiting Mike?"

"Tomorrow," said Dave.

"You going too, Tom?"

Tom looked to Dave who said, "Yes."

"Take care, please. Both of you." Then she was gone.

10

Mike Davidson

When Tom went back to their house at nine on Saturday morning Brandon was not home. Whether he'd ever returned after the night out was unclear: there was no note saying what he was doing, nor had the shower been used recently. Without having a phone, there was little Tom could do, except assume his dad was at work. He was happy enough with that as it meant he could return to Dave's place and be with Buffy.

Mid-morning, Dave sent Tom and Buffy on a walk out to the road so Tom could spy on the subdivision. His job was to check if Mike Davidson was working on the block wall. He wasn't visible, but parked by the gate was a ute with dog boxes on the back. It had to be his.

Three more visits were needed before Tom could report back that the ute had gone, suggesting Davidson had finished for the day. Now was the time to visit Bush Road.

Sitting beside Buffy in the cab, Tom's anxiety became more intense the closer they got to the turn-off. While the three encounters he'd had with Mike Davidson had been friendly enough, this was an altogether different situation. Dave's silence suggested that he too, was nervous about what might happen.

Once again Dave drove to the locked gate before turning around and driving back. This time he stopped and parked the ute on the verge outside the house. Buffy was already barking, as were the dogs from the shed in the back. Davidson's vehicle was parked in the carport.

"Quiet, Buffy," commanded Dave. "You're staying here until we sort things out." Then he looked at Tom. "Wind the window down a bit to let in some air. I'm locking up. Just in case."

With that done, they moved down the track around to the back door. Surprisingly, the barking from the shed had stopped. Dave knocked on the open door, stood back and waited.

First out was a dog, similar in breed to Harvey, except taller and nowhere near as fat. The growling suggested it was also meaner. Tom took a couple of steps backwards. Then a woman appeared and shouted, "Shut up, Spot." Instantly, the growling stopped and the tail-wagging began.

"He's all noise," explained the woman. Two young children came out the door to stand beside her. "He's the kids' dog. Far too spoilt he is. Anyway, how can I help you?"

"Mike home?" asked Dave.

She nodded towards the shed. "He's feeding the dogs. You can go down if you want."

Thanking the woman, they moved off.

The shed was shaped like a small barn, with open doors in the middle of both ends. Storage cupboards and shelves lined one side, and there were five dog cages on the other, four of them with a dog in each. The cages were filthy, as if they hadn't been cleaned for days. To Tom it seemed as if the only time the dogs got out was when Davidson went hunting.

No wonder Buffy likes being with us, he thought, staying close to the door to avoid the stench.

The four dogs were each feeding from a bowl. Mike Davidson was leaning against a centre pole facing the door as if expecting them.

"You're the one who drove past the other day," he said. "Wondered when you'd be back." There was a hint of suspicion behind the words.

Dave stepped forward with his arm extended. "Dave Hughes," he said.

Davidson shook the hand before turning to Tom. "Hi Tom," he said. "How come you're with this man?"

"Dad's at work. Dave's looking after me."

"You're big enough to look after yourself, aren't you?"

Tom shrugged. "Dad says I'm not."

Davidson turned back to Dave. "What is it you're after?"

Dave waved his arm in the direction of the pens. "You've got an empty cage. Is one of your dogs missing?"

For several seconds it seemed as if Davidson wasn't going to answer. Then he said, "Could be. Why? You found one?"

"Yes. A greyhound-cross by the looks of it. Grey and tan bitch. She yours?"

"Yeah, that sounds like Lucky. When did you find her?"

"Monday. Her GPS collar was caught on a broken branch. She'd tried to get free and rubbed the skin on her neck raw."

"You got her with you?" asked Davidson.

Dave nodded.

"Then let's go get her." He took a step towards the door.

"Not yet," said Dave. "There's something we need to talk about."

Davidson stopped, turned, and gave a sneering smile. "I get it," he said. "You want a reward."

"No. I want to talk about that GPS transmitter you had on her."

The sneer turned to a snarl. "What about it?"

"It's an American one. That frequency's illegal in this country. Did you know that?"

"So what? Doesn't cause any harm."

"Yes it does. It's the same as the forestry uses. You're interfering with their traffic."

"I don't go hunting when they're working."

"They say you do. Your dog was certainly there at the same time they were."

Davidson changed tack. He gave a sheepish grin. "Yeah, I suppose it does happen sometimes." He spread his arms wide. "Okay, I'll make sure it doesn't happen again. Now can we go and get Lucky?"

Dave shook his head. "Not yet. I want to talk about those new batteries you put in."

"What!" said Davidson. "This is crazy."

"Not crazy at all," replied Dave. "The battery was ready to explode. Which it did when we took it out. What if that had happened when it was still on the dog? That wouldn't be 'crazy', would it? That would be cruelty, maltreatment, abuse. You choose the word."

Davidson's face darkened. "I do not abuse any of my dogs."

"Yes, you do. Every time you put one of those collars on a dog, you're close to setting fire to them. Give me the collars and I'll give you your dog back."

"This is all bull," shouted Davidson. He began pacing around the barn. "I don't have to take this nonsense. Some one-armed freak comes on to my property, accusing me ..." He stopped and turned to Dave. "You want abuse. I'll give you abuse. Get off my property. Get off, or ... or ... Just get off."

Now Dave was equally angry. "Or what? Or you'll start shooting? Like you did over Dargaville way."

This took a moment for Davidson to process. His eyes narrowed. "Yes! That's not a bad idea." He moved to one of the cupboards at the side and began fiddling with the lock.

"That's right, get your gun," said Dave, not letting up. "I hear you talk big about shooting things. Kiwi killers and the like. Well maybe you need to take the gun to one of your own dogs."

Davidson, who was about to pull the cupboard door open, froze. "What was that?"

"You heard. If you want to shoot a kiwi killer, this shed is a good place to start."

"Jeeze, you really are crazy," said Davidson, throwing open the door. "Well I'll soon fix—"

"STOP IT!"

The two men turned to stare at Tom who was standing rigid, his arms stiff and tight by his side, his whole body shaking.

"Stop it!" he said again, slightly quieter. "Stop it." This last one was a cry.

Then he ran.

He burst out the door, across the yard, out to the road and towards the gate. There was no thought to where he was going. He just had to run. Run from the fighting, the arguing, the yelling. Where, didn't matter, as long as it was away from the shed, away from everybody, away from it all.

When he did stop running, he found he was deep in the forest. He must have climbed the gate, but had no memory of doing so. Nor did he have any sense of how long he'd been running, either in distance or time. This part of the forest was much steeper than where he normally ran. The road was narrower with a steep bank rising on one side, and a sharp slope, almost a cliff, falling away on the other.

Looking upwards to the narrow strip of sky visible between the tree tops, he saw the blue was changing to orange towards the east. Somehow, a couple of hours had passed since they'd set off from Dave's place. Another hour and it would be dark.

Turning back was not an option. Back was where things went wrong. The only way to go was forwards, following the track towards the setting sun. Sooner or later it would link up with a road that he recognised, one that would take him home.

Being in the forest, listening to the birds sing their last songs for the day, would normally have been enjoyable. Not on this day. He'd calmed enough to think clearly about the events in the shed, and to figure out his chances of keeping Buffy. They were slim. The bottom line was that Mike wanted his dog back, and Dave was prepared to do that in exchange for the illegal collars. All the other accusations were just angry talk. Once the men calmed down they'd come to an agreement. Chances were it had already happened, and Buffy was back in a filthy pen, known once more by her old name of Lucky.

"Lucky?" Tom asked of the forest. "What's lucky about living in a cage all the time?" In answer the birds paused their singing for a while. Long enough for him to hear the whisper from the top of the pines moving in the evening breeze, but that still told him nothing. He continued on his journey.

Moping and walking. He'd done a lot of that in his life. It always seemed that when something good was happening, it was taken away. The first week of these holidays had been one of the best ever. Now, with Buffy gone, the second week would be back to the boring stuff. He might as well be down in Hamilton with his mum. At least there they'd give him some money; living with his dad he didn't have enough to even go to the movies. But what did it really matter: without Buffy, he'd be lonely in either place.

These thoughts continued until an over-powering smell of death dragged him back to the present. *Another dead kiwi?* he thought.

Actually, it was two of them, a father and a chick. Their bodies lay on a carpet of pine needles at the bottom of the steep slope beside the track. The needles made the surface too slippery to investigate closely. Anyway, there was no need. The injuries were the same as they'd seen with the kiwi by the pond, a week before. A dog had done this. A dog had come all this way into the forest for the single purpose of killing. This had nothing to do with food, with the need to stay alive. These birds were killed for one reason only – for pleasure.

Looking around, Tom wondered how many other dead kiwis there were in the forest. So far, the ones that had been found were always close by a road or track, the easily accessible ones. But the dog could have roamed anywhere. There could be dozens of others, in amongst the trees, maybe hundreds.

Then he saw another one, further along the road, that he could climb down to. When he did, the first thing he noticed was that the smell was different: not of death, but something else. What was it? Something to do with cooking, maybe. Then he had it: one of Brandon's favourite breakfasts was mushrooms fried in butter. The kiwi had the same smell as mushrooms that had been kept too long in a plastic bag. This had to be the smell people talked about, the one that was so attractive to dogs.

Then another thought came: did it mean the kiwi was freshly killed?

Yes it did! The blood around the wound was also different, red not black, and there were no flies. It had happened that day.

Although Tom was saddened that yet another kiwi had been killed, this was mixed with a feeling of relief. There was no way Buffy could have been involved in this bird's death. She'd been with him all night and day up until when they'd arrived at the Davidson house, and even then she'd been locked away in the cab of the ute. She was in the clear. She was not the kiwi killer. Maybe life wasn't so bad, after all.

His spirits rose even higher over the next twelve minutes. The first five of those he was travelling downhill to a junction with a road that he recognised. The next five were walking along that road, knowing he was heading in the right direction. The final two good minutes came after he saw the headlights of a vehicle flickering between trees as it travelled towards him. Hopefully it was Dave coming to rescue him. Only after the vehicle pulled alongside did his emotions take a downward dive. And this time they fell all the way down to deep bottom.

The ute *was* Dave's, and Dave was the driver. However nobody else, human or canine, was with him. In the space to the left of Dave, where Buffy should be, was a cardboard box, filled with a jumble of collars and electronic gizmos. Tom knew then that his fears had become reality – Buffy's freedom had been swapped for a pile of dangerous junk.

11

More Misery

"What do you want done with this?"

These were the first words Tom had spoken since Dave had picked him up in the forest. They were back at the house and the 'this' was the box of collars.

"Put them in the shed," replied Dave. "I'll deal with them Monday."

"What if they explode?"

"I think it only happens when they're moved around a lot. Anyway, the shed's all metal. They're not going to cause too much damage." Then he smiled. "But you'd better carry them carefully."

Tom didn't smile back. He was still angry with Dave for what had happened to Buffy.

The shed was tucked away against some bushes behind the house. Inside were metal shelves holding a few tools, and a lawnmower with a can of petrol. Tom put the box on a top shelf well away from the mower and the petrol. If a battery did catch fire then the roof would get a bit hot, but that would be all.

Dave was on the phone when he got back to the house. Tom noticed that Buffy's bed, food bowl, and water had already been removed. It was as if she had never existed.

When the call finished, Dave said, "That was your father. He'll be late home tonight, so you need to stay here."

"Aw, no," moaned Tom. Every other night he'd stayed at Dave's he'd had Buffy to make sleeping on the sofa bearable. "Do I have to?"

Dave sighed. "Yes. You know you're not to be left by yourself."

"When's he coming home?"

"He said he'll be home before I leave in the morning."

"What time's that?"

"I'll be getting up around five."

Tom almost let out another groan. That meant he'd have to get up at the same time. "What if he's not home by then? He doesn't always do what he says, you know."

Dave thought about this. "Tell you what, Tom. You can have my phone for the day. I won't be needing it, they don't work in the forest. Then if anything goes wrong, you can ring your dad and he can sort it. You do know how to use a phone, don't you?"

"Duh," said Tom, pulling a face.

"Yeah, all right. Point taken." Dave moved to the coffee table against the wall. "I'll put it on the charger now, so it's here if you need it. Okay?"

Tom nodded. The thought of having use of a phone for the day brightened his mood a little, but nowhere near enough to make up for the loss of Buffy.

As expected Brandon wasn't there when Tom went home shortly after five o'clock on Sunday morning. Not that this worried Tom. He crawled into his bed determined to sleep all day if he could.

Hunger woke him around lunchtime. In the meantime Brandon had been back and gone again. He'd even left a note.

I'll be home around five. Pizza tonight as usual?

Tom could have done with a pizza right then. Instead he went to the fridge to see what was left there. Nothing. *Dave will have something.*

As usual, Dave had a well-stocked fridge. Tom decided to make the next best thing to a pizza – cheese, bacon, and tomato, grilled on toast, which he ate sitting in front of Dave's television.

After that he thought of going for the long ride he'd

planned for the weekend but, somehow, he couldn't raise the energy. His attention drifted from the television to Dave's phone, which was likely to be much more interesting than the dumb comedy he was watching.

The first thing he noticed when the display opened was the message icon showing two unread text messages. Tom's finger hovered over the icon for a moment, before his brain issued warning signals about prying. The finger moved to the Google Earth icon instead. Soon he was looking at a satellite image of Waitangi Forest. From it he was able to trace the route he must have taken from the Davidson house through the forest. He could even identify the steep bit where he'd seen the dead kiwis. This gave him an idea.

Getting the phone number for the local DoC office was easy, making contact with a human was not. A recorded voice told him the office was closed on a Sunday, however a message would receive attention when the office opened on Monday. Tom told the machine about the dead kiwis and their location, reading the GPS coordinates from Google Earth. As he was ending the call, the phone vibrated in his hand. Another text message had come through. This time the first part of the message appeared on the screen so he couldn't help but read it.

Hughes, I want my gear back, you …

Is that Mike Davidson? thought Tom. *Maybe the other messages are from him too*. This time he did tap the message icon. Yes, all messages were from the same sender. No name showed, only the number. He couldn't read the full messages without opening them, but he could see all three had abusive swear words.

Tom had no doubt the messages were from Mike Davidson, and that the man had not willingly handed over the tracking gear. Clearly the matter was far from over. In a strange way, that pleased Tom. If the man wanted his gear back, maybe the swap could be reversed, and Buffy could become his again.

The rest of the afternoon was spent at home playing games on Dave's phone. Just after five o'clock he heard a vehicle moving along the track. Maybe his father was on time for a change. No, he wasn't. When the vehicle got closer the sound was all wrong, and it continued past their place to Dave's – it must be him who had finished for the day.

After half an hour Dave's vehicle left again. *Maybe he's gone out for pizza too*, thought Tom. Then he realised how disastrous that could be. If Mike Davidson got pizza every Sunday night, then there could be a fight right there in the shop. The same thing could happen when Tom went too. Suddenly the taste of pizza was no longer so attractive. He picked up the phone and rang Brandon.

The phone rang and rang before it was answered. Even then Brandon sounded distracted.

"Dad, Tom here."

"Yeah, okay. I'll be home soon. We'll get pizza as usual. See ya."

"No," said Tom quickly. "I don't want pizza tonight. Let's have Indian." Indian food was Brandon's favourite.

"Yeah, all right. I'll pick you up soon."

"Why don't you bring it home. It'll be quicker that way."

After some thought, Brandon agreed and the call ended. One looming crisis averted. However, there was nothing Tom could do about the other one. If Dave was going to the pizza shop, he'd already be there. Tom returned to the game.

The first to arrive at the house was Dave, and he was angry.

"Have you been home here all day?"

"No, I was over at your place for a while."

"So it was you who made all that mess?"

"I only made lunch. It wasn't much … I was going to go back—"

"Not much!" yelled Dave. "I'd hate to see what you thought a real mess was."

Tom opened his mouth to speak, before thinking better of it. From past experience he knew how futile it was to argue with a tired, angry adult. Nothing good ever came from it. "I'm sorry," he said. "I'll go and clean up now."

Dave calmed a little. "No, leave it. You can come over in the morning." He scanned around the house. "Where's Brandon."

"Collecting dinner, I hope."

"Have you been here by yourself all day?"

Tom nodded.

"Has he been working?"

"I don't know."

"Well, what else would he be doing?"

Tom kept his mouth firmly shut. If he voiced his suspicions, it might make them true.

"All right," said Dave with a sigh. "When he *does* come home tell him I need to see him. I've got to work again tomorrow. Ray's mother has taken a turn for the worse. I'm filling in." He paused. "You got my phone? I'd better put it on the charger. You can pick it up when you do the cleaning. No need to get up early, though."

As soon as he had the phone, Dave checked his messages. His body stiffened as he read the first one, and remained that way as each of the others was opened and read. Before he could make comment, the sound of Brandon's van indicated dinner had arrived.

"Good," said Dave. "I'll talk to him now."

They waited in silence until Brandon breezed in.

"Ah great," he said. "I thought you might be here, Dave. You like Indian? There's more than enough for everyone." He put two bulging plastic bags on the table, and turned to them with a big grin. Only then did he notice the grim faces. His jaw dropped. "What?"

"You said you'd be here to look after Tom," said Dave.

"Yeah ... well ... something came up."

"What?"

Brandon squirmed. "Um ... just some business."

"What business is more important than your son?"

"Yeah, yeah. I know."

"So where were you?"

No answer.

"He was at the pub," said Tom. "That's where he always goes."

"No!" shouted Brandon. "I was not at the pub. I don't do that any more."

"Then where were you?"

More squirming. "At the arcade," he mumbled. "Playing Gods of Zuron."

"What!" said Dave and Tom together.

Brandon tried a grin that didn't work. "It's a console game. There's a group of us play online. We're pretty good."

"And you call that business?" said Dave with a sneer.

"Yeah. We make money out of it. As I said, we're good."

Dave shook his head in disbelief. "You can make money from playing computer games?"

"Yes," replied Brandon, gaining in confidence. "You can make thousands."

"So how much did you make today?"

"Ah, it doesn't work quite like that. Some of the games can take days to finish. This one will last a bit longer. But we're winning."

Dave stared at him. "Brandon, you need to take a good look at what you're doing, mate. You're letting people down. You let Tom down all the time. You're always late and he has no idea what's going to happen from one day to the next. And today you let me down. You said you'd be home here with Tom and you weren't. What would have happened if something had gone wrong, eh? You could have got both of us into a hell of a lot of trouble."

"Yeah, nah," said Brandon looking at the floor. "I know I got it wrong. It won't happen again.'

"Well, we'll soon find out," said Dave. "I have to help out again tomorrow, so you've got Tom."

"Um ... ," began Brandon. "That's bit awkward. I just got a call asking if I could start at first light in the morning. Boss wants us to finish picking before the storm comes through in the afternoon."

"So when can you get back?"

Brandon shrugged. "Lunchtime?"

Dave thought about that. "All right. Tom will have my phone so he can call you if there's an emergency. Is that okay Tom?"

"Yeah, I'll be right."

"And you," said Dave, pointing a finger at Brandon. "You keep your word. Stop playing computer games and start being a father." And with that, he left.

12

DNA Results

When Tom woke on Monday morning Brandon had already left. A note outlined his intentions for the day.

> I've arranged to finish work at midday. Remember, you can use Dave's phone to call me at anytime if something comes up. I should be home by midday. See you then.
> P.S. I think we should get you a phone. Maybe do it this afternoon. What do you think?
> PPS. Don't use the Indian for breakfast or lunch. We'll have it for dinner tonight.

Tom read it a couple of times: this was more detailed than any previous note from his father. Maybe Dave's harsh words had achieved something. That thought, along with the idea of getting his own phone, immediately raised his spirits. He decided to start the new week with a run: this one would be running for enjoyment, not away from an argument.

For the first time in weeks, the sky was not wall-to-wall blue. High clouds glowed red with light from the rising sun, a sure signal trouble was on the way.

He chose the same run as the previous Monday, the one to the truck roundabout where he'd discovered Buffy. Although he told himself it was the best run to do in the morning, deep down he wished he could turn back the clock and Buffy would be sitting there, waiting for him.

She wasn't. Even so, he sat on a log catching his breath and listening to the sounds of the forest. The bird calls were more subdued than usual, more like chatty chirps than joyful songs. Perhaps the birds could also read the danger signal in the sky.

This time, the noise from the tree tops was the howl of the strengthening wind, which also carried sounds from the logging operation where Dave was working. The roar of multiple chainsaws suggested a rush to fell the remaining stands before the winds made further work impossible.

There was no sound of a dog whining, of course, and nor would Tom have wanted to hear it. If Buffy couldn't be with him, then shut away in Davidson's shed was as good a place as anywhere to survive the coming storm.

On the run back home, his thoughts were interrupted by the sound of a vehicle coming from behind, a diesel engine but smaller than a logging truck. He stopped running, moving to the side of the track to let it pass. When it came into view he recognised the dark green markings of a DoC vehicle. At the wheel was Sally Page, the woman who had visited Dave's place the week before. *The authorities.*

She pulled up alongside. "Getting your run in before the storm?"

He nodded.

"I've been collecting those dead kiwi you reported yesterday."

Tom's eyes widened. He hadn't left his name, had he?

Sally chuckled. "I recognised your voice." Then more seriously, "You don't have to be scared of us, Tom. We're here to help."

He remained silent.

"But it would have helped if you'd told us about that injured dog when I called last week. We could have started the tests earlier. That would have helped a lot."

Tom froze, thinking, *The killer's Buffy.*

Sally went on. "You see it would have allowed us to eliminate her straight away."

"How?" he asked, his eyes growing even wider.

"Because at that stage we already knew from the DNA on

the kiwi that we were looking for a male dog, not a bitch."

Tom let out a long sigh. "So all my worrying was for nothing," he said, mostly to himself.

"Not exactly," said Sally. "I gather she's still unregistered and unchipped."

"What are you going to do?"

"I'll pass it on to the local dog enforcement officer. But the best thing would be for you to take her in and get her registered before he calls. She'd get a chip and then you'd be all legal."

"Except," said Tom, sighing, "she's been taken back by the owner."

Sally nodded slowly. "And you're upset about that?"

The smallest of nods.

"Who is the owner?"

Tom's first thought was to remain silent. Then his mind began working overtime. If Buffy was taken away from Davidson, then that would allow him to go to the pound, claim her, get her registered, chipped, and then she'd officially be his dog.

"Mike Davidson," he said.

Sally grunted. "Why am I not surprised?"

Tom had another thought. "Did you DNA check his dogs?"

She shook her head. "No. He's too far away from where the kiwi were killed."

"No, he's not," said Tom. "His house is quite close to those I found on Saturday."

"Yeah, I suppose the road does turn back in." She thought for a time before adding, "Anyway, it doesn't matter now. The results have come through and we know who the killer dog is."

"You do! Who is it?"

"Aw, I can't tell you that, Tom. We've got to go through a process. All I can say is we'll be picking the dog up later today." She patted the box on the seat beside her. "And that will mean no more of these dead kiwi." Then she sighed. "But that's only until the next killer comes along."

Tom had even more things to think about when he resumed his run. Top of the pile was the big question: whose dog was the killer? The only other dog he knew in the area was Harvey. Could he really be the killer? He did attack moving things such as bike wheels. But it was a big jump to go from there to attacking kiwi. One thing he knew for sure was Mrs Hopwood would be devastated if it turned out it was her dog.

As usual, thinking of kiwi killers soon had him seeing shapes in the undergrowth. He rejected them as fantasy until one shape seemed to be moving, running along parallel. Then he got a clear view for a fraction of a second. It was Harvey.

"Harvey," he called, slowing to a walk.

The dog also slowed.

"Come here."

Now it stopped and turned towards Tom.

"Come here, boy. You need to be taken home."

Harvey raised his head, sniffing the air."

"Yes. It's me, Tom. Come on."

The head went higher, revealing a small patch of white on the chest, a feature Tom hadn't noticed before.

"Come on, Harvey, let's go," said Tom, resuming the run. "Go, go, go!"

This time Harvey did move, but not to follow Tom. He moved deeper into the shadows, disappearing from view.

Tom kept running, deciding that he'd better let Mrs Hopwood know. Even if Harvey wasn't the killer, he was certain to be picked up if Sally Page saw him running loose.

Harvey still hadn't come out of hiding by the time Tom got to the main road. Pausing to check for traffic, he noticed Mike Davidson was working on the concrete posts to the fence, fixing hinges in place. The temporary gate had been moved to one side. On the back of Davidson's ute two fancy wrought iron structures were taking the space where the dog boxes normally sat. Mrs Hopwood was finally going to get a proper gate.

With Davidson around, there was no way Tom was going any closer. Harvey would have to remain free. Anyway, he wouldn't be harming anything, would he? Probably just getting a bit of self-exercise. Tom turned and ran back home.

After a shower and late breakfast, Tom went over to Dave's place to do the dishes he'd left in the sink Sunday lunchtime, the 'mess' that Dave had got so upset over.

Taking the key from under the steps, he unlocked the door. That's when he saw what Dave had been complaining about. The place *was* a mess, with furniture in the wrong places, chairs toppled over, cupboards left open. It had not been like this when Tom left the day before. Someone else had been inside between then and Dave arriving home.

As Tom restored order, he thought about why someone would want to mess up Dave's house. Could it be that the man had lots of enemies? Or was there only one – Mike Davidson? With this thought in his mind, he began to see that the mess might not have been created out of spite – someone could have been searching the house. And, if it *was* Davidson, then Tom knew exactly what that man would be looking for.

A quick trip out to the shed confirmed his suspicions: the box of tracking gear was no longer sitting on the top shelf.

Back in the house, he considered what he should do. The man might be going on a hunting trip, and that would put the dogs in danger. Tom had to try and get them back.

One idea was to go to the subdivision and confront him. Better still was to sneak over and see if the box was still in Davidson's ute. However the chances of approaching the ute without being seen were slim. Unless Davidson could be distracted in some way.

Alongside Dave's phone on the charger was a local phone directory and Mrs Ellen Hopwood was listed. Tom rang the number.

"Mrs Hopwood, it's Tom here."

"Oh, hello Tom. Did you get your bike fixed?"

"Yes thank you. Um ... did you know that Harvey is outside your gate, over in the forest?"

A sigh. "So that's where he's gone. I did see the gate had been moved. That horrible man is working again."

This was the opening Tom had hoped for. But just as he was about to talk of a distraction, another thought jumped into his head. Something that had been puzzling him.

"Harvey's got a white patch on his chest, hasn't he?"

"A white patch on Harvey?" asked Mrs Hopwood, mystified. "No. He doesn't have one. I've seen Labradors that do, though. Why do you mention it?"

"Oh ... um ... I must've been mistaken." Before he could say anything more a beeping sound came down the phone.

"Ooh, that's my timer," said Mrs Hopwood. "My biscuits are ready. I've got to go. Why don't you come over later and have some?"

Tom mumbled that he might and disconnected. His mind was racing. The dog he'd seen in the forest definitely had a white patch, spot or blotch on its chest.

Blotch, patch or spot? Did it matter what you called it?

Yes, it most certainly did. He'd met a dog named Spot recently. The Davidson kids' dog was called Spot. The dog he had thought was a skinny version of Harvey.

13

Killer Revealed

The rain began at 12:47. Tom knew this exactly because he'd been watching the time on Dave's phone and Brandon was already 47 minutes late. He planned to give him half an hour before he phoned and complained.

He'd returned to their house before midday so he'd be there when Brandon arrived. He planned to convince his father to go out and buy a phone straight away.

While he waited, he used Dave's phone to research the various models and packages. He didn't want a prepay as he'd always be begging his father for money. He wanted a monthly plan, one that Brandon couldn't get out of easily. Two gigabytes of data would also be ...

These thoughts were disturbed by the sound of a vehicle; not the rattle of Brandon's van, but the purr of something much more expensive.

He went to the door and saw a large SUV had stopped short of the grass. Mrs Hopwood was climbing down from the driver's seat. She walked towards the house, oblivious to the rain. Tom stepped aside to let her in. As she passed, he saw she was crying; not gently weeping, but howling noisily as if in pain.

"What is it?" he asked, unsure how to cope with a distressed woman.

She recovered a little and managed to say, "They …," before breaking down again.

Half a minute passed before she recovered and tried again. "They've taken Harvey away." More sobbing. "They say he's the kiwi killer."

Tom's hands went to his face. This was bad. Almost as bad as it being Buffy. How could it be Harvey? He was such a great dog – apart from attacking bicycle wheels – but to him, that was a game.

"Is that what the DNA says?" he asked.

"So they say."

After staring at each other in shock for some time, Tom realised she had come over for his help, and he should do something. What was it adults did in times like this?

"Would you like a cup of tea?" he asked.

She gave a little nod.

"Okay, I'll make one. And … um … you can sit down if you like."

Tom welcomed the chance to move into the kitchen and be busy. While he'd not made tea before, he'd seen it done: teabag and hot water, maybe sugar and milk. He'd better check.

"Do you have milk in it?"

"Yes please, but no sugar." She sounded as if she was recovering.

By the time the drink was made, she was mostly composed.

"Sorry there's no home-made biscuits," he said, placing the cup on the coffee table.

She gave a tiny smile. "I should have brought some over."

He waited until she'd taken the first sip. "Who came?" he asked. "Was it Sally Page?"

"It was a woman. She said she was from DoC. I didn't get her name. She already had Harvey in a cage."

"Did she get him outside the gate?"

"Yes-s-s." She'd started crying again. "That ghastly man helped her. He was still there, with her. Talking about shooting Harvey, he was."

"They won't let that happen, will they?

"I don't know," sobbed Mrs Hopwood. "The woman said they had to do more tests."

Tom grabbed at this. "So they're not sure it's Harvey?"

"They know it's a Labrador and Harvey's the only one that's in the area. She said they had another dead kiwi and hope to get a better sample from that. But she seemed pretty certain it was Harvey. She said there had been lots of reports of him roaming the forest."

"Did she say who by?" asked Tom.

"No." She looked up at him. "You didn't, did you?"

"No!"

"But you've seen dogs in the forest?"

Tom nodded.

"One with a white blotch? Is that what you were talking about this morning?"

Again Tom nodded.

Mrs Hopwood brightened. "Do you think you could catch that other dog?"

"Yes," replied Tom without hesitation. "I think I can."

"Oh Tom, please do. Maybe Harvey has a chance after all."

After Mrs Hopwood had left, Tom rang his father, not to complain, but to tell him that he wouldn't be home most of the afternoon. As it happened, Brandon didn't answer, which made it easier. Tom left a message saying he was going out, without giving further details.

The short ride to the main road was mostly sheltered from the rain, which was now being driven by a strengthening wind. Crossing the road was difficult with gusts forcing him sideways. Fortunately there was little other traffic.

Mike Davidson was no longer at work. According to Mrs Hopwood, he'd left in a rush straight after Sally had taken Harvey away. Before going, he'd shifted the two wrought iron gates from the ute to where they now leaned against the wall, one each side of the open gateway. With Harvey gone there was no need for the temporary gate to be back in place.

Tom's wind jacket was already soaked by the time he settled to a steady speed, moving eastward towards Bush Road. He had no plan for what he would do when he got there, other than to try and grab Spot and hide him in a safe place. The way Davidson had rushed home the moment he heard that a Labrador was the killer, was mighty suspicious, almost as if he knew his dog was the real culprit. Tom feared that Davidson would make his dog disappear, rather than have people know that he'd covered up for a kiwi killer. Unless Spot was found and tested, Harvey would be the dog that faced the consequences.

When Tom got to Bush Road, there was no doubting the storm had arrived. The rain was pounding into his body driven by a wind that was almost impossible to ride against. It was slightly easier once he turned onto the gravel and was riding with the wind for a while. Already the drains at the side were overflowing and in a couple of places the water joined across the road.

The first thing he noticed when he got to the house was the ute was not parked in the carport. Tom's hopes rose a little. Maybe he could get Spot without having to meet Davidson. He leant his bike against the dog box dumped alongside the carport, and went to the back door.

Mrs Davidson opened the door almost as soon as he knocked. The two children were with her, but not Spot.

"Mike's not home," she said in a shaky voice. "He's gone out."

Tom quickly decided the best approach was to come out and say what he wanted. "I'm not here for Mike," he said. "I've come for Spot."

Mrs Davidson studied him for a while, long enough for Tom to think he'd made the wrong move.

Then she sighed. "I think you'd better come inside."

"I'm dripping wet."

'Hold on," she said. "I'll get some towels." The door closed.

It turned out that the towels were not for Tom to dry himself, they were to lay on the floor. When the door opened again there was a pathway of towels through to the kitchen. Once there Tom was handed a towel to dry his face. While he was doing this, Mrs Davidson shooed the children into the lounge, telling them to go watch television.

"Tom, isn't it?" she asked.

"Yes."

"Okay Tom, if you want Spot, you'll have to go into the forest because that's where he is. He escaped sometime during the night and was missing this morning when we got up."

"He's done that before, hasn't he?" said Tom.

"Yes," she said, sharply.

"And Mike knew about this?"

"Yes! Yes! Yes!" she shouted, so suddenly that Tom jumped. "God, I'm so sick of all this about dogs. Yes, that dog goes into the forest, and yes, Mike knew all about it. But he would never admit that *his* dog might be the killer. Never, not until you people came on Saturday. Then he said that he needed proof. So that's what he's doing now."

"How?"

"Yesterday he put one of the transmitters on Spot so he could track where he went."

Tom nodded slowly. "So that's why he stole them back." He said this more to himself than to the woman.

"Oh, he would never have given those up for good. They're his favourite toys."

"So Spot is in the forest with a transmitter?" asked Tom.

"Yes. So is Mike. He's in there with the direction finder looking for Spot. He said he was taking another dog with him."

"Which dog? Was it Buffy, I mean Lucky?"

She paused. "Yes, I think it was her. She's usually the only dog he lets out. She often plays with Spot. So he probably took her. All I know for sure is that he's in the forest and that's no place to be with this storm getting worse. I'm scared."

"Did he take a gun?"

"I don't know. He usually does."

"Have you told anybody about this."

She shook her head. "Only you."

"We should tell the police."

"No! That's the last thing Mike would want."

"Then what are we going to do?"

"I don't know," she said, quietly. "Wait, I suppose. Wait until the storm is over."

Tom shook his head. Not him. He wasn't prepared to wait. If he waited Spot would disappear and never be found. Harvey's only chance of survival was if Spot was kept alive. If one was buried, then so too would be the other. And then there was Buffy. Who knew what the man had planned for her?

14

Emergency

The first thing Tom did after his discussion with Mrs Davidson, was to check the barn to see if Buffy had been taken. She had, and so too had another one: Davidson had two dogs with him. The remaining three jumped up in their cages, barking, seeking attention. For a moment he considered taking one of them with him, but quickly dismissed the thought – none of them looked anywhere near as friendly as Buffy.

However he did search through the cupboards until he found a bundle of dog leads that might prove useful. He stuffed one in his pocket, and after a bit of thought added an old collar. The gun cupboard alongside was locked so there was no way of checking whether Davidson had taken one or not. Chances were high that he had.

Before leaving the shelter of the barn he rang his father once more. It went straight to voicemail suggesting the phone was turned off. After leaving a message he stood for a while wondering what else he should do before heading into the forest. Should he tell someone else where he was going? Yes, he should. He selected Marika's number.

After bringing her up-to-date with what had happened, he told her he was going into the forest to find Davidson.

"No!" Marika shouted down the phone. "It's too dangerous. MetService have updated the storm warning. The winds are coming sooner than expected, and they'll be much stronger. That forest is no place to be in a storm like this."

"I've got to," cried Tom. "He's going to shoot Spot and Buffy's with them!"

Marika took her time before replying. "Look, why don't I contact the logging gang, and see if they can do something. They know the forest better than anybody."

"But phones don't work in there," said Tom. "That's why I have to go."

"I know that," said Marika, patiently. "I'll contact the company in town here. They have radio communication with the site. Just stay where you are, Tom. Don't do anything until I call you back. Right?"

Before Tom could respond she'd disconnected.

While he waited for a return call, Tom marched up and down the middle of the barn becoming increasingly worried about the time he was wasting.

When the call did come, he answered it with a rude, "So?"

"They can't make contact," said Marika with a sigh. "There's something interfering with their signals. They're very—"

Tom broke in. "That's the dog collars. I can stop that when I find Davidson. Don't you understand? That's why I have to go in. I'm off now."

This time it was Tom who disconnected before there could be any response.

The gate into the forest was open which saved a bit of time. The track was awash with water, making it impossible to tell whether the ute had come that way or not. Tom assumed it had, otherwise the gate would be shut.

Pelting rain lashed at his back until he got into the shelter of the forest. From there on the riding was a little easier, but the storm no less scary. Roaring noises coming from the tops of the pines made it seem as if jet planes were flying low overhead. Even the tree trunks close to the ground were swaying with the force. Tufts of pine needles flew everywhere, grabbing at his clothes as they rushed past.

Tom really had no plan other than to follow the road until he found something, whatever that might be. He thought he was ready for anything, but when he turned a corner and found a dog rushing towards him, the shock made him swerve far too sharply on the muddy road. His tyres lost traction and the wheels slipped sideways. Both bike and rider crashed to the ground. The next moment Tom was fighting off the dog, which was attacking his head, its open mouth searching for his throat. Tom screamed, wrapping his arms around his head, curling into a ball.

That worked. The dog pulled away. When it started whining, he took a peek through his fingers. The dog was sitting, staring at him in shock. This was no wild animal, it was Buffy! The attack had not been aggression, just welcoming joy, her way of cuddling. Now they had both calmed down, their reunion was more orderly. For a while they hugged each other. Two wet and muddy beings, happily oblivious to the storm raging above them.

Tom's first thought when they eventually separated was to forget about Davidson and take Buffy home. His home, not that stinky barn Davidson thought was suitable for a dog. However Buffy had other ideas. As soon as he'd climbed to his feet, she was pulling at his shorts, with the clear intention of taking him somewhere. After realigning the handlebars and untwisting a brake cable, Tom got on the bike, and followed her command.

Further along the road they came to the first fallen pine tree. This one had been growing at the top of a clay bank which had collapsed, dropping the tree across the road. The dirt still falling from the exposed roots suggested it had happened in the last few minutes. Tom stopped short of the barrier and glanced upwards at the remaining trees swaying dangerously above him. For the first time since entering the forest he experienced a surge of fear. If he'd not fallen off his bike he could well have been under the tree when it fell.

Climbing over the barrier was not all that difficult; getting his bike over was. He considered leaving it behind until he realised how that would leave him without any quick way out of the forest if things went wrong. He hauled his bike over and obeyed Buffy's urges to continue.

A kilometre further on they rounded a bend to find the road blocked by another fallen tree, this one much smaller. Buffy could have easily leapt over the thin trunk, but made no attempt to do so. Instead she moved to where the top branches dangled over the edge of the road, and stood staring at something below. Tom's stomach lurched when he saw wheel tracks leading over the edge: a vehicle must have come round the bend, swerved to avoid the tree, and gone over the edge.

Before he'd got off his bike to join Buffy he was already picturing what he would see at the bottom of the slope. This time the rush of fear almost forced him to retreat.

When he did make himself look over the edge, it didn't seem too bad. Yes, the ute was down there and it had crashed into a tree, but only the front was dented. The driver's door was open a little, although not enough to see if someone was still inside.

Tom studied the surrounding area looking for Davidson. There was nothing to indicate the man had left the vehicle. By then Buffy had begun climbing down the bank, looking back every few steps, whining at Tom to follow. He did so.

It soon became clear Buffy wasn't taking him to the vehicle, she was heading for a clump of ferns. Her whining got louder as they approached, this time directed at a black shape lying half hidden within the ferns. To Tom it looked like a black stump. That was until he was right above, and saw it was the body of a dog, the other one Davidson had taken with him. Unlike Buffy, this one was fitted with a transmitting collar.

Buffy crouched beside the body, resting her head on its flank, showing that she knew her pack companion was already dead. The only sign of injury was that the head lay at a strange angle, which made Tom think its neck might have been broken during the crash. While he could do nothing to help the dog, he should do something about the transmitter. The sooner it was turned off the better.

He was about to roll the body over when the horn of the ute sounded. Tom jumped with fright. Buffy barked, before taking off, racing towards the sound. Tom followed.

The horn was still blasting when he opened the driver's door. The cause was Davidson's body slumped across the steering wheel. Tom grabbed the shoulders and heaved them back. The horn stopped sounding. Tom pulled his hands away not wanting to touch the body any more than he had to. Looking down he saw Davidson's legs were crushed where the motor had been pushed back into the cab. A pool of blood had formed in the buckled floor. Even if the ute had been fitted with airbags, they wouldn't have saved him. Davidson had probably died from loss of blood.

Then, as Tom was thinking this, the man groaned. His eyes opened and his head turned.

"Tom?" he croaked.

"Yes it's me," replied Tom.

"What are you doing here?"

"I came to get Spot."

Davidson processed this. "So did I," he said. "So did I.

"Did you find him?"

"Sort of." His head turned to the seat alongside where a metal aerial lay. "That thing did."

"Where?" asked Tom.

But Mike's eyes had closed. The man had blacked-out again.

For a time Tom experienced a surge of panic that blocked out all sensible thoughts. He walked around in circles beside the ute, his head waving from side to side, arms dangling uselessly. "What to do? What to do? What to do?" he repeated over and over. Nothing had prepared him for a situation like this.

Eventually it was Buffy who brought him back to his senses. She stood glaring at him, barking noisily until he stopped pacing.

"What?" he asked glaring back.

Her reply was a softer bark as she turned and trotted back to the dead dog.

Tom followed. "Yes, he's dead. I can't do anything about that. I've got to work out what to do about Mike."

Buffy began nuzzling her dead pack companion, whimpering quietly. That's when Tom remembered the transmitter. This time he did turn it off. That would help radio communications a bit. But the one on Spot would still be causing problems. Should he find Spot and turn off the collar, or should he go get help for Mike.

He turned to the dog. "What should I do, Buffy?"

Her answer was a gentle woof.

"That's no help," he said.

He tried to think it through. The logging site was the closest place. Would it have a first-aid kit? Yes, it was sure to have one. If he went there somebody could come and deal with Mike, while he and Buffy found Spot, and turned off the transmitter. Then an ambulance could be called.

"Yes, that will work."

Another woof.

"Yeah, yeah, I know. How will they find Mike?"

A louder bark.

"Noise! That's how. Thanks, Buffy."

He rushed to the ute and fished around in the rubbish on the floor. Mike had said he had lots of bungees, was there one here?

There wasn't, but there was one on the back. It took a while to get it tied tightly around the steering wheel. Then, all he had to do was jam a block of wood under it, and the horn was blasting.

Mike stirred at the noise without opening his eyes.

Encouraged by the signs of life, Tom turned to the dog. "Okay Buffy. Let's save this man. It's time to go find some help."

15

Help

The amount of debris on the forestry road had thickened in the time Tom had been at the ute, with still more falling. So much rubbish was catching in the spokes that, after a couple of minutes riding, he abandoned the bike and began running. Although he had to jump and dodge a lot, the going was faster and soon they were at a T-junction with the main forest track.

He stopped to check if the horn from the ute was still blasting. It was barely audible, fading in and out against the roar of the storm raging in the treetops. They moved on, heading left towards the logging site.

At the top of the first rise, Tom paused again to listen for the horn. That's when he heard a truck further ahead, grinding its way up a hill. From the growl of the engine it was fully loaded with logs, which meant it was coming his way, and soon he'd have to get off the road to let it pass.

He was about to resume running when he had another thought. Maybe the driver could help Mike. Were they trained in first aid? He'd have to stop the truck and ask. But where should he do that? Not on an upward slope, because the truck would never take off again. Downwards wouldn't work either as the driver would be trying to pick up speed for the next hill. The top of the hill would be the best place. He decided to stay put and let the truck come to him.

Tom and Buffy took shelter against the trunk of a pine tree. The rain was even heavier than before with water pouring off the slopes to form streams down the wheel tracks of the road, washing away most of the debris.

Minutes passed as the truck continued climbing the hill. Then the growl lowered in pitch, and got louder when it reached the top. Scanning through the trees, Tom was relieved to see the glow of headlights, confirming it was heading his way. Another couple of minutes and it would be alongside.

The noise from the truck changed to the ripping sound of exhaust braking as it headed downhill. Then came other noises, crashing, trees being broken, metal being scraped. The braking ceased, the engine roared, then died completely, until there was only the howling storm.

"Come on, Buffy. We've got to go," cried Tom.

At the start he raced down the slope, his heart pounding faster than his legs. But he soon had to slow or he too would crash as his feet slipped and slid in the mud formed by the streams. At the bottom, the water had pooled forming a pond filled with debris from the trees. Buffy was through in a shot, racing up the other side. Tom was slower, aware he'd be no use to anybody if he also became a casualty.

The crash scene was not as bad as he'd imagined. The tractor unit was mostly still on the road, except it was leaning against the branches of a couple of trees. The passenger side of the cab had been crushed during the impact. The driver's side was fine, with the driver still seated behind the wheel staring down at Tom. At the rear, the trailer had skidded and jack-knifed, coming to rest with the back set of wheels hanging over the drop on the other side of the road. The logs had shifted but were still in place. Although everything seemed stable for the moment, anything could happen if more water came down the road.

Tom climbed onto the step, and opened the driver's door.

"You okay?"

The man gave a weak nod. "Yeah, mostly."

"Do you want a hand to get out?"

"Nah, I'll be all right." The man gave a big sigh and straightened up.

Tom stepped down so the man could get out.

After he'd done a few stretches to check everything still worked he turned to Tom and asked, "Who are you, anyway?"

Tom introduced himself.

"Hi Tom, I'm Jay. What are you doing in here?"

Tom explained about the ute crashing, finishing with, "Do you have a first-aid kit?"

"Yeah. I'm trained." Jay climbed back into the cab, found the kit, and handed it down. "I better call this in before we leave. That's if the radio's working."

Tom waited, hoping the collar he'd turned off might have made a difference. A minute later, Jay's swearing from the cab told him it hadn't.

Jay climbed down. "Something's stuffing up the radio."

"I can fix that," said Tom. "I know what's causing it."

Jay stared at him. "Tell me."

Tom told him about the illegal collars.

"Mike Davidson, eh?" said Jay at the end. "I've not met him, but I've heard of him. Nothing much that was good." He thought for a while. "So you reckon you can find this dog and turn off the collar?" A nod. "How?"

Tom pointed down to Buffy. "Using her. I think she can track him."

Jay climbed back into the cab again. When he reappeared he was carrying the radio unit. "Just as well these come out easily. You turn off that collar and I'll be able to call help."

He paused. "I hope." He fiddled with the unit. "Yep, the emergency battery's okay." He turned and surveyed the scene, shaking his head. "There's nothing we can do here without help. C'mon, let's go."

At the T junction they parted, Jay to follow the sound of the horn which was still blasting, and Tom to follow Buffy who wanted to head along the main track towards town. Hopefully she was tracking Spot.

All was well for a few minutes with Buffy trotting along nose to the ground. Then she stopped, unsure of where to go.

"Come on, Buffy," encouraged Tom. "Find Spot. Where's Spot."

In answer she moved into the forest following some sort of trail. Apparently that went nowhere, because she returned and headed in another direction. Tom was beginning to wonder if Spot's scent had been washed away by the rain when, suddenly, she made up her mind and took off so fast that she was soon out of view.

"Wait!" shouted Tom as he headed in the same direction. "Buffy, wait!"

She did. From there on she moved quickly, while checking every few metres that Tom was still following.

They were moving through mature forest that would soon be harvested. The undergrowth had been undisturbed for almost 30 years allowing ponga ferns to grow taller than Tom. In places the ground was completely covered with shrubs. There were tracks of a sort, although far too small for a human. Tom wondered if they'd been made by pigs. Was that what Buffy was following? A pig track? After all, she was a pig dog.

The further they went, the more Tom became sure they were on the wrong track. But what else could he do except follow.

On and on they trekked, Buffy sure about where she was going, Tom increasingly doubtful. When they moved into an area which had been dug up by pigs, his confidence hit rock bottom. This was an absolute waste of time.

Buffy sniffed around the area for a while, looking up at Tom as if expecting him to be pleased.

He wasn't. "No Buffy," he growled. "Find Spot!"

In answer she raised her nose to the air, sniffing noisily.

"Yes Buffy. Get Spot!" encouraged Tom. "Go! Go! Find him!"

Buffy took off. This time there was no pausing to make sure Tom was keeping up, she pushed through the undergrowth leaving him to scramble as fast as he could. Fortunately the race didn't last long before she moved into a clearing and there, at the edge was Spot, his nose deep into a burrow, his paws frantically digging trying to make the hole bigger.

"Aargh!" yelled Tom long and loud as he raced at the dog, his arms stretching out to grab him by the collar.

He managed to get one hand on it, before Spot reacted. The dog's head whipped around, ripping the collar out of Tom's fingers. The jaw opened, thrusting forward. Tom backed away, his eyes wide with fright. Never before had he seen a dog this mad.

With several metres between them, boy and dog faced each other, Tom breathing heavily, the dog snarling through bared teeth. That's when Buffy decided to get involved, creeping forward, barking noisily.

Spot turned away, unable to maintain eye contact.

"Wait, Buffy," said Tom. The last thing he wanted was for Spot to be scared off. That dog had to be caught.

Buffy and Tom stood, waiting to see what Spot would do next. He returned to digging up the burrow.

Tom stepped closer. "No Spot. No! Leave!" When that had no effect, he took another step forward, and another. Now he was close enough to touch the dog, but he held back, unwilling to risk another attack. Again he yelled, and again Spot kept digging. So frantic was the action that steam was rising from the dog's neck.

No! That wasn't right. Not from his neck. This was coming from the collar. Water had got into the battery. The thing was about to explode. He needed to try something different.

"Help me, Buffy," he cried. "Grab him! Hold Spot!"

Buffy moved closer, unsure of what was expected of her. Tom took a collar and lead out of his pockets, clipped them together, and mimed putting it on Spot. Buffy moved forward.

By then steam was jetting out of the tracking collar. Spot must have felt the heat for he pulled his head out of the hole and shook it. Tom leapt onto his back, reaching forward with the lead, hoping to get it in place while Spot was distracted. He got it around the neck before the dog reacted, but it was still not tight enough. Spot was writhing so much, trying to get his teeth at Tom, that it was near impossible to stay on his back. This wasn't going to work.

That's when Buffy joined in. She leapt forward, grabbed Spot by an ear and held him, much the same as she would hold a pig during a hunt.

That was all it took. Tom got the collar in place. Now he had to remove the transmitter.

"Keep holding him, Buffy," Tom cried, as his fingers fumbled with the buckle. And then he was screaming as flames spurted out of the battery alongside his bare left arm. He pulled back with so much force that, miraculously, the buckle came free. Still screaming with pain, Tom ripped the burning transmitter off and threw it as far away as he could.

Yet, even with that out of the way, Spot couldn't be released. He needed to be tied up. Working together, Tom and Buffy hauled him to a broken branch lying nearby. Tying the end of the lead to the branch was not easy with Tom's left arm near useless with pain. Even when he'd finished Tom wasn't sure it would hold if the dog really wanted to go, but he'd had enough. He collapsed to lie flat on the ground.

Buffy also released her hold, but instead of lying down to recover, she stood over Tom, barking frantically.

"What is it, Buffy?" he asked without opening his eyes. A paw scraped over his chest. This time he sat up. "Yes, what is it?"

Buffy was staring over top of him to where he'd thrown the transmitter. Pine needles were burning. Tom let out a cry of anguish. Now he had to put out a fire.

However, when he got to the flames, he found the fire was mostly dying by itself. The intense heat of the burning battery had reached down through the moist needles to set fire to the dry underlayer. With the fuel from the battery gone, the needles were now smouldering rather than burning.

Two minutes of stamping around with his feet had it under control. Although smoke and steam were still rising, Tom was confident that the pouring rain would eventually put it all out. For him, the emergency was pretty much over.

Sure, he still had to make his way back to the main track, but for now he would sit down and take a rest – his first in the last three hours.

16

Kiwi

Time passed without Tom really noticing, as he sat in the forest recovering. He'd found a place where water had pooled, unable to soak into the dry soil. With his burnt forearm resting in that, he felt little pain unless he moved – another reason for not getting up and leaving.

At the start Buffy had sat staring at him, trying to force him into action. When this didn't work she moved off to explore their surroundings. Spot was crouched down looking sad for himself, knowing he was in deep trouble, waiting for the punishment to come.

Tom must have dozed off, because when Buffy began barking he came to with a jump. She was standing, staring down into the burrow where Spot had been digging.

Oh no, not you too.

"Out of there, Buffy. Leave."

Buffy moved back a little before crouching down, whining noisily while still staring at the burrow.

"What is it?" said Tom, climbing painfully to his feet. "Can you see the kiwi? Is that what it is?"

It was, and when Tom peered down the hole he could see it too. What he also saw was that its breast feathers were stuck together with blood – Spot's teeth or claws had made contact with the bird.

Tom had to lie on the ground to reach it, and even then he couldn't get two hands under the body. By feeling around he got hold of a leg and pulled. The kiwi fought but somehow that made it easier, and soon he had the bird on the surface.

Spot barked when he saw it, pulling on the lead until he had the branch moving. "No!" shouted Tom. "You've done enough damage." Still Spot kept pulling, until Buffy turned and snarled at him. Then he backed away a little.

Examining the kiwi, Tom found a single gash on the breast that had ripped back the skin, exposing the flesh. With treatment the bird might survive; without, it was sure to die. But Tom had no idea where they were, so how could he guide Sally Page or any other rescuer to this place? Leaving the kiwi here wasn't an option, he'd have to carry it out, and that posed a problem. With his injured arm there was no way he could carry the bird, and control Spot on a lead at the same time.

The solution was to connect the end of Spot's lead to Buffy's collar. At first Spot pulled on the lead trying to get free, but a couple of snarls from Buffy soon had him under control. With them settled, Tom folded the bottom of his jacket up over the kiwi, and instructed Buffy to find the main track. If he could make it there, then help shouldn't be far away.

The trip out seemed to take forever. Going in, Tom had been spurred on by the need to find Spot. Now, there was not the same urgency, plus he was exhausted. So much so, that a couple of times, he stopped to lean against a tree trunk, not sure he could go any further. It was Buffy who got him going again. She seemed to have taken on responsibility for everyone – Spot, the kiwi, and especially Tom. With each step, the bond between dog and boy grew stronger.

During the trek, the storm passed its peak, allowing other sounds to be heard. A few birds ventured out and began calling in the late afternoon. Then came the sound of a siren, and Tom knew they were close to the main track. A few minutes later they pushed through the undergrowth onto the firebreak alongside the road. The source of the siren had passed by, but that didn't worry Tom – it would have to come back the same way, at some stage. He sat down to wait.

Help, when it did arrive, came without sirens or flashing lights. That made no difference to Tom, who wouldn't have heard or seen them anyway. He'd passed out, his body toppled over onto the road, arms still embracing the kiwi. Buffy was standing guard with Spot crouched down as far from the others as the lead would allow.

Fortunately Marika Greenwell was wide awake, excited about the story she was chasing. When the lights of her SUV picked out the group on the road she slowed to a stop and turned on the emergency warning lights. Buffy was at the door before she had it fully open.

"Hello Buffy. Is he all right?"

In answer Buffy led the way over to Tom who was still unconscious.

"Tom? Tom?"

His eyes opened. "I'm here," he said weakly.

"Are you injured?"

"Yes."

"Where?" Then Marika saw the bulge at his waist. In the dim light it looked like some horrific injury. "Oh my god! Your stomach! What happened?"

Tom gave a feeble smile. "No, that's a kiwi. It's my arm that's injured. Can you give me a hand up."

Once standing, Tom showed Marika the kiwi and its injury.

"Did a dog do that?" she asked.

Tom nodded.

Marika's eyes went wide. "Buffy?"

"No. That one there," said Tom pointing to Spot who was cowering in the shadows. "He's Spot, the Davidson's pet dog."

"Is he now," said Marika, thinking. "Um … do you mind if I take some photos … like … before I take you to hospital?"

"Yes please," said Tom. "I want everyone to see what the real kiwi killer looks like."

The next 12 hours were hazy for Tom. He remembered helping the dogs into the back of the SUV before climbing in himself and also the difficulty of fitting the seatbelt while he still held the kiwi. After that were bits and pieces at the hospital: his burn being treated, some injections, and the transfer into a bed. From then on there was nothing until he woke to find it was daylight outside, with blue skies. His father sat beside the bed, working his phone.

"Hi Dad,"

Brandon looked up, startled. "Oh! You're awake. How do you feel?"

"Okay, I guess."

"How's the arm?"

Tom looked across to his heavily-bandaged left arm, which was arranged out to one side, lying on a pillow of its own. "Don't know. Can't feel a thing." He wriggled his fingers. "It still works, but."

"You had quite an adventure," said Brandon. "Didn't you."

Tom shrugged. "Where were you when I called?"

"Working. The boss wanted to get most of the fruit in before the storm hit."

"But the storm had started by then."

"Um ... yeah, nah, we were in the shed sorting out what we'd picked. The rain was so heavy I didn't hear the phone. Sorry Tom."

Another shrug from Tom. Maybe it was true, maybe not. "So what's been happening," he asked.

Brandon brightened. "Well, you're a bit of a hero around here. What with saving Mike Davidson, a kiwi, and bringing in a kiwi killer. Everyone's impressed."

"Is Mike okay?"

"He's in here somewhere," said Brandon, waving an arm. "I hear his legs are pretty banged up. Won't be going pig hunting again in a hurry."

"What about the dogs? What's happening to Buffy?"

"I dunno," said Brandon, without interest. "I suppose they're in the pound."

Tom thought about this. Maybe now was the time to say what he wanted, while Brandon was all defensive. "I want Buffy to be my dog."

Immediately Brandon began shaking his head. "Aw, Tom, I don't know about that. Your mum won't want a dog around the baby."

Tom glared at him. "But I'm living with you!"

Brandon turned away. "Your mum's making noises about having you back … back with her in Hamilton."

"Why?"

"You'll have to ask her that. She'll be here later."

After his father left, Tom had little time to think before a nurse arrived to change his dressing, take his temperature, and generally check him over. Then a junior doctor came and gave him the once over. After that there was food, of which Tom ate about half.

He had just settled down again when Dave Hughes arrived to pick up his phone. They found it in the bedside cabinet. Dave checked it was still working before bringing Tom up-to-date with what had been happening.

"That logging truck's been cleared off the road and they're working at the site again. It'll take the rest of the week to process all the trees they felled. But they saved most of them. Only a few came down with the wind." He paused to shake his head. "I can tell you it was pretty rough in there at the height of the storm." He chuckled. "But I don't have to tell you that, do I? You were there at ground zero. Bit of a hero aren't you?"

Tom deflected the comment by asking about the dogs.

"They're in the pound. That DoC woman … um, Sally … she went and picked up all of Davidson's pack. They're being tested to see if any of the others are also kiwi killers."

"What will happen to them?" asked Tom.

"Well, I doubt they'll ever be returned to Davidson. None of them were registered or chipped." A pause. "I've got in mind to try and get one of them myself."

"Buffy?"

Dave smiled. "No, you'll want Buffy, won't you?"

Tom looked away, not wanting Dave to see the tears that were forming.

"What's the problem?" asked Dave. Then, when Tom wouldn't answer, he said, "Aw, I get it. You're going back to live with your mum. Is that it?"

Tom gave the slightest of nods.

"And you don't want to go?"

"No."

"Well, don't give up yet. You never know what might be possible. Just hang in there, Tom, and I'll see what I can do."

Next visitor in line was Marika. She had news on the kiwi, which had been all sewn up and was doing well. She repeated what Dave had said about Mike Davidson's dogs, and then she gave news about Mrs Hopwood's dog, Harvey.

"He's not been fully cleared yet. He'll be held at least until the DNA results come back for Spot. But that's simply a precaution. Sally Page no longer believes Harvey's the killer."

She then moved into a full interview about the events of the previous day. Tom answered her questions, but his mind was elsewhere, thinking of the future rather than the past.

At the end, she said, "By the way, Mike asked me to tell you he'd like to see you sometime. He's at the other end of the ward. I gather he wants to thank you." She smiled. "I wouldn't mind being there for that. Get a photo of the hero meeting the villain." The smile faded. "But that's not going to happen, is it? Mike Davidson is not a happy man."

After she left, Tom decided he'd go meet the man, and get it done with. He needed to get out of bed and go to the toilet, anyway.

Mike was asleep when Tom arrived, but it was obvious why he was not a happy man – he was hung up by cords like a puppet. Both legs were plastered and raised up from the bed. His chest was tied with a bandage, and blotches of antiseptic paint covered other parts of his body. Even in his sleep he looked angry. Tom decided to leave and come back another time.

On his way back, Tom explored the hospital. He discovered there wasn't much to it, and it wasn't even in

Kerikeri. It was in Kawakawa, an hour's drive from home. Tom then realised that Dave had gone out of his way to visit, it wasn't just a courtesy call, it was the action of a true friend. Maybe the man really could do something about keeping Tom with his father in Kerikeri.

That hope was shattered soon after he got back to his bed. In the seat was his mother and standing, with the baby in a sling on his chest, was the partner, Allan.

Mandy's first words were, "So, this is the mess your father got you into."

Tom climbed into his bed before speaking. "Hello Mum. How are you?"

"I'm all right," she snapped. "More importantly, how are you?"

He shrugged. "My arm's sore, but the rest of me is okay."

"What I want to know is what were you doing out in the forest during a tropical cyclone?"

So Tom told her.

When he'd finished she said, "Some people are calling you a hero." Her voice had softened. "Sounds like you were."

"I don't know about that."

Then the hardness came back. "What was your father doing all of this time?"

"He was at work."

Mandy snorted. "So he says. I'd like a second opinion on that. I know him from old."

"He's not like that any more," said Tom, hoping he sounded convincing.

Another snort. "Oh yeah? What is he like?"

"He's changed. He's more settled."

"Yeah, right," said Mandy, her voice full of sarcasm. "I suppose it's a change if you're not living in the back of a van any more. But that hovel he's got is no better. No son of mine should live in a place like that. When you get out of here you're coming to live with me."

Tom opened his mouth to object, but Mandy shouted him down.

"No! No argument, Tom. That's what's going to happen. I've made up my mind."

This time Tom jammed his mouth shut. There was no point in arguing when she was in this mood. Instead he looked up at Allan to see what he thought of the move. But the man had turned his back and was staring out the window, his body tight and motionless. He clearly didn't want another man's son living in the same house, and that gave Tom a glimmer of hope. Maybe, sometime later, when the couple were alone, Allan would do the arguing for him.

17

Keri Keys

When the doctor did his rounds on Wednesday morning, he gave Tom the all clear to go home. While waiting for Brandon to arrive, Tom walked down the ward to see Mike Davidson.

He found the man awake, lying back on the pillow, staring at the ceiling.

"Hi Tom," he said without enthusiasm. "I hear you're leaving today. How's the burn."

"Still hurts. How are your legs?"

"They're stuffed. Be months before I'm back at work. Don't know what's going to happen with my business in the meantime."

"Can you get somebody else to do it?"

"That's what I was thinking about." He sighed deeply. "Anyway, I wanted to thank you for what you did ... like ...

in the forest. They tell me things could have ended up … well, a lot worse if you hadn't come along. So thanks."

Tom nodded his acceptance.

Mike continued. "I suppose you know what's happened to my dogs."

"I heard they're in the pound."

"Yeah. I can't see why they have to take all of them. Those dogs are like family to me."

Tom pictured the conditions in the shed where the dogs had been kept. *Yeah,* he thought, *pity you didn't treat them that way.*

The man moved in the bed so he could look directly at his visitor. "Tell me, is it true you found Spot actually attacking a kiwi."

"Yes." Tom went on to tell him exactly what he saw, and what happened to the kiwi. By the time he finished, Mike was shaking his head from side to side.

"He wouldn't have learnt to do that by himself. No dog of mine would attack kiwi without help. Some other dog taught him that. I bet it was that mongrel, Harvey. He was always in the forest. He's the real killer. I reckon they had the right dog all along." He paused, before adding, "That was until you started interfering."

Tom's jaw dropped, his eyes wide. This guy was in total denial. He would blame anybody and anything rather than accept his own dog was a kiwi killer. Tom had actually been feeling a bit sorry for him, but now ... now he was speechless. But even if he could've found the words, he knew they would have been wasted on this man. The best response was to walk away, which was what Tom did.

The remainder of the school holidays passed slowly for Tom. His arm was still too sore to ride or run, and he'd lost his enthusiasm to train for the triathlon. He knew he wouldn't be in Kerikeri much longer. Nothing had been decided yet, but the signs were bad. Each night after dinner Brandon rang Mandy. He did it outside, so Tom couldn't hear what was going on. But Tom knew they were arguing, and he also knew that when it came to arguments, his father never won.

There was a bright spot on Saturday when Brandon bought Tom a phone – exactly the model and deal Tom wanted. That filled in the rest of the weekend. Even so, Tom was relieved when school resumed on Monday, and there were other things to help fill in time.

By Tuesday Brandon was back into his old habits, arriving home late without any explanation of what he'd been doing. The phone discussions with Mandy continued.

Wednesday was much the same. Then, on Thursday Brandon texted while Tom was at school.

Won't be home for dinner tonite. You'll have to find your own way home. I've contacted Dave. He's expecting you.

Tom was more than a little annoyed by this. Yes, it was better than not knowing what was happening, but only just. He began to understand why Brandon had been so keen on buying the phone – it allowed him to stay away from home longer.

When Tom knocked on Dave's door he was surprised to hear a whole lot of barking from inside. Was this Buffy? His hopes rose. Had his father organised this as a surprise?

No such luck. When Dave opened the door, the dog that came out was not Buffy, although it certainly looked like a pig dog.

"Hi Tom. Come in and meet Charlie. He was one of Davidson's pack."

Tom was shocked. "Why didn't you take Buffy?"

"Aw, a bitch can be awkward. Unless you want to breed they can be a real pain."

When he got inside Tom saw Buffy's bowl and bed were set up next to the couch. Already Charlie had taken the place of Buffy, and that hurt.

Over dinner Dave told of the latest developments. The DNA testing proved that Spot had been the killer of all the kiwi. Harvey had been cleared and returned to Mrs

Hopwood. Spot had already been euthanised. The rest of the Davidson pack would be sold to recover costs. Any that didn't sell would go the same way as Spot.

Tom had listened in silence until this last bit, when he couldn't control himself any more. He stared at Dave in horror. "You mean Buffy could be put down?"

Dave shook his head vigorously. "No Tom. She's already gone. Someone else took her."

"Who?"

A shrug. "When I got Charlie yesterday, she'd already been taken. They said it was to a good home. I'm sure it was. They check new owners very carefully."

That calmed Tom a little.

Later, when they'd done the dishes, he sat on the floor and played with Charlie, except it wasn't the same as being with Buffy. After 20 minutes he thanked Dave and went home to bed.

Over breakfast on Friday morning Brandon said they were going to Mrs Hopwood's for dinner that night.

"I didn't know you knew her," said Tom.

"I didn't until she came up to me in the supermarket, when you were in hospital. She asked how you were getting on."

"You never said."

Brandon shrugged. "I forgot, I guess."

"So when did she ask us to dinner?"

"Um ... she sent me a text yesterday. We're to be there by five. I'll pick you up from school. That'll give us plenty of time to get ready."

Tom was still puzzled, unable to figure out why it had taken Mrs Hopwood almost two weeks to make contact. And even then it was with Brandon, not him. At first, Tom had expected her to visit the hospital, and when that didn't happen, he'd hoped she'd come over to the bach. At one stage he'd considered going over to see her, except that would be almost like skiting about what he'd done, so he left it for her to make the first move. And now she had, although it did seem a rather strange way of doing it.

At exactly five o'clock Brandon and Tom walked over the road to the new development, which now had a flash nameplate attached to the block wall – Keri Keys it was called. Someone had also finished installing the gates. As they approached, these swung open to let them through.

"How did that happen?" asked Tom.

"They're automatic."

"Yeah, I know. But how did they know we were here?"

"Ellen must be watching through the security camera."

Tom wasn't convinced. His father's manner was a little too accepting. Something was going on here.

Harvey met them halfway down the driveway, his tail wagging so much that his whole body moved. Behind him were Mrs Hopwood, along with Marika and Dave. Apparently they were invited to dinner as well.

After they'd all greeted one another, Mrs Hopwood suggested they do a tour of the development. They started with the houses which were now close to being finished. Then they moved down to where the development met the inlet, a part Tom hadn't seen before. He found this much more interesting than the houses. There was a jetty, a boat ramp, and several mooring buoys, one with a launch attached. A dinghy was resting upside-down on a small beach. The area would be a great place for kids to play.

From there they moved up to a smaller house, tucked away at the back of the development. Mrs Hopwood insisted they take a look around inside. Tom tagged along, even though he would have preferred to go back to the estuary.

They did the lounge, the kitchen, the laundry, the bathroom ... and it all looked great, but of absolutely no interest to Tom.

Down the hallway were two bedrooms, one with its own bathroom. The second was smaller and as boring as any other empty bedroom. Tom had moved away to walk down the hall, when he heard his name mentioned. He turned back.

"What was that?" he asked.

Mrs Hopwood was grinning at him. "I said, this will be your bedroom."

"Eh?"

Mrs Hopwood chuckled. "This house is where you'll be living."

Tom turned to Brandon who was also grinning. "Yes, we'll be living here. This is the caretaker's cottage and I'm the caretaker."

By then everyone was grinning except Tom.

"When did this happen?" he asked.

"Over the last week," said Mrs Hopwood, "although I'd been thinking of it for some time. I asked around and found people had good things to say about Brandon, especially his boss. So I approached him when you were in hospital. Over the last few days we've been visiting plant shops sorting out the landscaping, and today we signed an employment contract. He starts Monday."

Tom shook his head as if to clear it. He still wasn't convinced this was all good news. "Does Mum know about this?" he asked.

"Yes," said Brandon, "and she approves."

"But does she approve of me staying in Kerikeri?"

"Yes. She does now that I've got a permanent job and a decent place to live. We have a new custody agreement. I'm now the main caregiver. That was signed yesterday."

Tom stood absolutely still for a time, letting that sink in. The others waited.

"Okay," said Tom almost to himself. "Does this mean I can have a dog?"

Brandon looked at Mrs Hopwood and then at Dave to see who would answer. In the end it was Mrs Hopwood who spoke.

"You already have one, Tom. Take a look out the window."

The first thing Tom noticed was the pen tucked against the corner of the block wall. It was made in the same style as the gates. Inside the enclosed space was a green kennel. Standing in the kennel was a dog. Not just any dog. It was Buffy. When she saw Tom she began jumping up and down with excitement.

While Tom struggled to regain control over his emotions, Mrs Hopwood explained. "Buffy is my thank you present for what you did for Harvey. The pen was Dave's idea and was paid for by the logging company. I've built one too for Harvey. Buffy won't have to stay in there all the time, only when you're at school, so she can't go wandering across to the forest." She held out an electronic remote. "This opens her gate. You can go out and see her now if you wish."

Without speaking Tom moved out of the bedroom, down the hall and outside, forcing himself not to run. When the pen came into view he saw that Buffy was now standing by the gate. She understood what was happening.

He stopped and pressed the button on the remote. There was a clunk as the magnetic lock released. Buffy's excitement went up another notch. She already knew what that sound meant. Next came the whirl of a motor, followed by the gate slowly opening outwards. This was nowhere near fast enough for Buffy. She began squeezing through, even though there was scarcely enough of a gap for her nose. For a moment her rear end jammed, then she was free, bounding towards Tom, braking just before she would've crashed into his legs. She looked up at him, mouth open, tongue waggling, eyes glowing, more excited than he'd ever seen her before.

Tom lowered himself to his knees, his eyes already moist. Then he put his arms around Buffy's neck to hold her tight against his chest. Tears streamed down his face. Not tears of pain or distress. These were different. These were the first tears of joy he could ever remember. And yet, somehow he knew, right then, they were unlikely to be the last.

Authors Note

I have seen kiwi in wildlife parks and zoos on many occasions, but only twice in the wild: once on Kapiti Island and again on Stewart Island. I think it sad that the bird which most often identifies New Zealand and New Zealanders is so rarely seen in its native habitat.

Sure, they are nocturnal animals which means they will be difficult to find, but a major pest – the possum – is also nocturnal and most us will have seen them many times. The problem with kiwi is that there are so few of them; yet that is something we can alter, if we have the will to do so.

When I was young, tui were birds that you saw mostly in the bush. Now they are commonly seen in cities, even in the most built-up parts. This change was achieved by planting trees for the tui, along with creating conservation areas that made it easier for birds to move from one place to another. In Wellington much the same has been achieved with our native parrot the kaka. I believe that if we set our mind to it, we can achieve similar changes for kiwi. The first step would be to better control the introduced pests that prey on all of our native birds

In July 2016 the New Zealand Government announced a goal of making the country predator-free by 2050. The main targets would be rats, possums and stoats. These mammals kill 25 million of our native birds every year, as well as millions of other native species such as lizards, snails and insects.

Also targeted would be feral cats which kill around 100 million birds a year, although not all of these are natives.

There are four goals for 2025:

- Having 1 million hectares of land where pests are suppressed or removed;
- The development of a scientific breakthrough, capable of removing entirely one small mammalian predator;
- To be able to demonstrate that areas of 20,000 hectares can be predator free without the use of fences;
- And the complete removal of all introduced predators from offshore island nature reserves.

For more information visit:

predatorfreenz.org

Noah Larsen's family has just moved to Stewart Island when he sees a spectacular parrot flying over the bush, a South American macaw, a bird that should never be in the New Zealand forest. Soon afterwards native parrots, particularly kaka, start dying. He and local girl, Hailey, suspect a visiting yachtie is responsible, but without proof nobody will believe them.

Then, when one of the last remaining kakapo becomes threatened with disease, Hailey and Noah must battle against both time and weather to capture the macaw. All the while knowing that if they fail, they will have aided the extinction of one of the world's truly special creatures.

AVAILABLE IN PRINT AND E-BOOK
FROM www.deshunt.com

After more than forty years working in education, Des Hunt is now a full-time writer living on New Zealand's Coromandel Peninsula. Since the 1970's he has shared his fascination with science and technology through textbooks, electronic devices, and computer programs. More recently he has turned to fiction as a way of interesting youngsters in the world that surrounds them. His first novel, *A Friend in Paradise*, was published in 2002.

www.deshunt.com